A Tense—and Tender—Moment

Susannah placed her hand upon the blue-coated arm, her gaze not directly meeting her escort's. "It is most kind of you to invite me to sup with you, sir."

"I will enjoy the company, Miss Brown. It is not often my table is filled with such grace and beauty."

Susannah flashed a questioning glance at her escort's face, but the smile he gave her was reassuring ... somewhat.

He then led the conversation into general areas, discussing literature, the weather, and even life on a country estate. Without realizing it, Susannah relaxed and responded to his gentle care, talking and eating more than she had in the past month. Even more amazing, she caught herself laughing at the squire's ridiculous tales of his children's exploits.

"What is it?" she asked when she caught him gazing at her strangely.

"I had not realized dimples must be added to your list of charms, Miss Brown."

Susannah blushed and turned away ...

Titles by Judy Christenberry

MOONLIGHT CHARADE
SWEET REMEMBRANCE
SUSANNAH'S SECRET

Susannah's Secret

Judy Christenberry

JOVE BOOKS, NEW YORK

SUSANNAH'S SECRET

A Jove Book / published by arrangement with
the author

PRINTING HISTORY
Jove edition / March 1993

ISBN: 0-515-11060-4

Jove Books are published by The Berkley Publishing Group,
200 Madison Avenue, New York, New York 10016.
The name "JOVE" and the "J" logo
are trademarks belonging to Jove Publications, Inc.

PRINTED IN THE UNITED STATES OF AMERICA

10   9   8   7   6   5   4   3   2   1

Susannah's Secret

1

The butler swung open the massive front door. A late winter wind whipped around the slim, cloaked form carrying a wicker basket.

"I've come to see Mr. Danvers."

Females did not often appear upon Nicholas Danvers's front step, as far as the squire's manor house was from any large town. The closest settlement was the little village of Bloomfield three miles away.

Nevertheless, Pritchard gestured for the woman to enter. He wouldn't leave anyone out in that sharp wind. If he didn't miss his guess, there'd be still another snowstorm this evening before spring would leave its calling card.

He pushed the door to and turned to find the woman still hidden beneath her garments, standing silently for his attention.

"May I tell the master who is calling?"

"I am Miss Brown." Her voice was so low, he bent to hear her words. "Mrs. Williams sent me from London about the post of governess."

Pritchard frowned. "We received no notice of anyone coming. We would've sent the carriage to the stage stop if—"

"I brought a letter," she interrupted, pulling a much-folded piece of paper from the side of her basket.

"One moment, please. If you would like, you may warm by the fire," he said, gesturing to the roaring flames in the huge fireplace farther along the entry hall.

He returned several minutes later, noting the young woman's bare hands stretched out to the flames. When he spoke, she whirled around, her blue eyes wide. Her hands immediately flew to the basket sitting in front of her.

"The master will see you now."

She stood, clasping the handle of her basket against her bosom.

"You may leave your things here. I will take care of them."

"No!"

Pritchard drew himself up to his full height. He was a strapping well-built man who ruled his domain supremely, and it was not often he was denied anything.

"Please. I meant no offense," the young woman swiftly said. "It is just—I must k-keep my basket with me."

"As you wish," he replied coldly, unmollified by her words.

He led the way to a room across the wide hall, swung open the door, and announced, "Miss Brown, sir."

The man behind the desk, even taller and more

muscular than his servant, rose as the slim figure entered the room. Her face was invisible in the brown woolen cloak, its hood drawn forward. He looked at his butler, wondering that the man hadn't taken the woman's outer garment. Pritchard shrugged his shoulders and shook his head.

"Bring us a pot of tea, if you please, Pritchard," Nicholas Danvers said as he came round the desk. "You are quite a surprise, Miss Brown. I only sent my request to Mrs. Williams three weeks ago. I confess I didn't expect any kind of reply for several months."

"I-I arrived at Mrs. Williams's office shortly after your letter arrived, sir. As I was in need of immediate employment, Mrs. Williams suggested I present myself for your consideration." It was a bold-faced lie. She hoped he wouldn't check her references.

"Of course. May I assist you with your cloak?" When she seemed reluctant to part with her outer garment, he added, "We'll sit here by the fire so you may warm. It is a bitter wind this afternoon, isn't it?"

Slowly, slender hands lifted the hood back from her head, and Nicholas almost gasped. The firelight flickered over the auburn hair, bringing it to life. The woman's porcelain-pale skin was colored only by scarlet cheeks and soft red lips. She lifted her eyes to his, and the picture of beauty was complete with her wide and fearful china-blue eyes.

Fearful? She must be nervous about the interview. But what was a young woman with her attributes doing applying for the post of governess miles from anywhere?

He took her cloak and reached for the large basket she'd set on the floor.

"No!" she gasped, grabbing the handle and pulling the basket up in front of her. "I-I must keep my basket beside me."

"Very well," he said calmly, but his eyes were narrowed in speculation. "I'll just lay your cloak over here." He put it across the horsehair sofa near the door and returned to gesture to one of the two wing chairs drawn up before the fire. "Won't you be seated?"

She lowered herself to the chair, which almost engulfed her entire being. Nicholas noticed she kept the basket upon her lap, but he said nothing, waiting for her to speak.

After a moment of consideration, she lowered the basket to the floor beside the chair and clasped her hands in her lap. She raised her eyes to his and gave a timorous smile.

This flawless gem of beauty was willing to bury herself in the country, miles from any entertainment, any shops? She was supposed to keep his boys in line? Nicholas Danvers almost smiled at the thought. His boys were his pride and joy, but even he knew they could be rascals. Her disposition seemed more suited to waltzing across a ballroom.

"Have you much experience with children, Miss Brown?"

The blue eyes were immediately hidden behind dark lashes. "No, sir, I haven't, but I like them."

Her ingenuous reply was the most amusing thing to come his way all afternoon, but Nicholas hid his smile behind his large hand.

"I see. And are you well trained in mathematics, literature, Greek, French, history?"

"I am well read in both history and literature, and I

am able to teach basic mathematics. I am quite fluent in French, but I am afraid I know no Greek, sir. Are your children quite old?"

Mesmerized by her red-rose lips, Nicholas had to force his gaze up to hers. "Um, no, not old at all. They are five and three."

"Oh," she replied with a sigh and a small smile. "Then I shall be quite able to teach them."

"They are both boys, Miss Brown, and quite—" He broke off as a low purr pierced the room. He frowned. He'd told Edward and Teddy they must keep their new kitten out of the library. He noted a look of frozen fear on Miss Brown's face. "Do not be concerned, my dear. My children have a new kitten. It must have found its way in here."

His words seemed to have little effect on the young woman, and he watched curiously as she stealthily slid her hand down to touch the handle of her basket.

"You have a fear of cats?" Though she shook her head fiercely, he was not convinced. "My children enjoy many pets, Miss Brown. Whoever becomes their governess must tolerate their whims. Within reason, of course."

"I have no fear of animals, sir," the young woman assured him, suddenly speaking rapidly. "Are there other qualifications?"

"Patience is always—" He stopped speaking as the mewing was repeated. "Excuse me," he said as he stood. Her large blue eyes followed his every move as he walked around the room, looking under furniture.

Pritchard's entrance with a tea tray, followed by a footman with offerings sent up from Cook, distracted Nicholas. The butler looked first at his master, standing by the window at the opposite end of the library from the young lady, and then at the female. "Is anything amiss, sir?"

"That dratted kitten has snuck in somewhere. I've heard it several times, but I cannot find it."

Pritchard gestured the footman to set down his tray. The two men joined the search for the missing animal. Nicholas Danvers, standing after looking behind the drapes, was surprised to see that anxious expression upon the young lady's face again. It only confirmed what he already knew. He would have to deny her the position. Anyone as inexperienced as Miss Brown would never be able to deal with Edward and Teddy. And he knew all too well that anyone as beautiful as Miss Brown would never be satisfied with life in the country.

"Never mind, Pritchard. It probably escaped when you entered. Remind the boys of my rule, please."

The two men withdrew, and Nicholas expelled a deep breath. His task would not be an easy one. "Miss Brown, do you have family in London?"

"No! No, I am all alone."

Damn. It would've been easier to give her a bonus and pay her way back home. "I doubt that you will be able to deal with my children. If the presence of a kitten frightens you—"

"I promise you, sir, it does not." The young woman leaned toward him. "I always had pets when I was a child. I would be—"

Another mewing sound, this one louder, interrupted her, and Nicholas watched in fascination as she froze. He frowned as her right hand stole down to the handle of the basket.

When she saw the direction of his gaze, she jerked her hand back to her lap. "I—I am quite exhausted by my journey, sir. Would it be possible to be shown to a room? We could continue the interview a little later." She paused and her eyes grew larger. "Unless you intend to send me on my way this afternoon?"

"No, of course not, Miss Brown. We are not exactly convenient to travel. You may stay for several days if you like. And we will discuss your filling the position later, if you still want to consider it. However—"

The shriek that rent the air had nothing kittenish about it.

All color fled from Miss Brown's cheeks, and she snatched her basket into her lap.

Nicholas Danvers, with an acute ear and aroused suspicions, did not search for the kitten any longer. "Miss Brown, what is in your basket?"

"My possessions, sir."

"Is one of your possessions alive?" he asked. As if in answer to his question, a wail arose from beneath the cheesecloth. Though Miss Brown clutched the basket to her breast, he managed to pull the cloth away.

A red-faced infant was snugly fit into the basket, resting on what appeared to be a pile of garments. The tiny fists waved frantically back and forth, and the wail that rose from the redbud mouth left no one in doubt of its unhappiness.

"Miss—Miss Brown, whose baby is this?"

All her bravado had faded. "My baby, sir," she whispered.

The squire, who had stood as he revealed the baby,

fell back into his chair, flabbergasted.

The baby continued to make its feelings known despite its mother's efforts to silence it. She lifted the baby from its basket and cuddled it against her. "I am sorry, sir. It is past her feeding time and—she is hungry." Miss Brown finished by sinking her teeth into her bottom lip in a futile attempt to stifle the sobs rising in her. Why couldn't her little one be silent just for an hour?

"Here now, Miss Brown," he said when he saw her eyes well. "I'll have Pritchard escort you to a room so you may—that is, so you may tend to the child's needs." Even as he spoke, he strode toward the bellpull.

Pritchard answered the summons at once, his curiosity roused by the strange young woman. However, he was unprepared for the sight that greeted him as he entered the library. "Sir, you ra— a baby!" The butler began to bend down to get a better look at the babe, but quickly realized his position and, with monumental effort, pulled himself together. "Yes, sir?"

The butler's struggles gave Nicholas time to regain his composure. "Would you please show Miss Brown to a guest bedroom and, uh, have one of the maids attend her?"

Pritchard approached the young woman, gesturing to the basket resting beside the chair. "May I?" he asked. She nodded and he bent gingerly to lift the now much lighter basket and led the way to the door.

Miss Brown stood, the baby held securely against her with one arm, and dropped a slight curtsy to the man now standing opposite her. "I am grateful for your forbearance, sir. I promise not to take advantage of your hospitality any longer than necessary."

Nicholas Danvers stood staring at the library door as it closed behind the trio. He surprised himself with a soft chuckle. At least the baby had proved that Miss Brown had no fear of kittens. But he thought there must be easier ways to demonstrate her tolerance.

When the butler quietly closed the door behind Susannah, she scarcely noticed the exquisite furnishings of the bedchamber. The child in her arms demanded her immediate attention. However, a rap on the door distracted her.

Without waiting for a response, a young maid carrying a tray entered the room, while someone unseen closed the door behind her.

"Evening, mum. I be Evie. The master said to bring you tea."

Susannah's tense shoulders slumped, and she leaned back in the chair. "Thank you, Evie. But I must feed my daughter first."

Evie moved to the chair to peer down at the baby. "My, she's a little thing. How old is she?"

"One month," Susannah whispered, amazed at how little time had been required to turn her world upside down.

"I brung you some fresh milk. My mam always said drinking milk when she was a-nursin' made for more milk for the young'in." Evie, who looked younger than Susannah by at least five years, took a maternal survey of her. "And you don't look that strong to produce enough milk for a mouse."

Susannah was touched by the maid's remark. "I promise you my child receives enough nourishment, but I appreciate your thoughtfulness."

The young maid sat down in a nearby chair and regarded the pair. Susannah, unused to being so closely observed, was at first tense, but Evie's friendly chatter disarmed her.

When at last the baby was satisfied and comfortable, Evie remembered her instructions. "The master said to put your little one in the nursery."

"That is most kind, but I must keep Cassie with me," Susannah said firmly, her full lips pressed tightly together.

"But, mum, there be no cradle here. You'd best let me tend to her. I helped raise nine brothers and sisters."

"I'm sure you're most capable, Evie, but my baby must remain with me. I will be leaving first thing in the morning, if your master will give me accommodation this night, so it does not matter."

"Well, at least let me put the babe on the bed while you have your tea. You must keep your strength up."

Reluctantly Susannah nodded. The girl walked across the room to the big bed and deftly covered the sleeping child with the comforter.

"Here. You've not eaten a morsel," she scolded Susannah.

Susannah took the glass of milk the girl handed her and sipped at the cold whiteness, surprised at how good it tasted. Her appetite had dwindled as her troubles increased, and her graceful slimness was fast approaching gauntness.

Evie spread butter on the fresh sliced bread, laid a piece of thinly cut ham across it, and handed it to her charge. When Susannah would've refused, Evie reminded her of her need to be strong for her child.

The heat from the fire as well as the food in her stomach had a soporific effect on Susannah, and soon her head was nodding as she fought to stay awake.

"Come on, now, lovey, let me tuck you up beside your little baby."

"No, I am not sleepy," Susannah muttered.

Evie rightly ignored her denial and pulled her from the chair. In no time at all, the lady and her baby were gently snoring in unison in the big bed.

Exhaustion and strain had taken their toll on Susannah, and she scarcely moved until Cassie's fussing woke her a few hours later. All was dark outside the window, and only a candle held back the shadows in the large bedroom.

"Oh, Cassie," Susannah said, sighing as she gathered the child to her. By placing several pillows behind her, she was able to suckle the child in comfort, both of them stronger because of the food and rest.

With tender fingers she smoothed the yellow strands on Cassie's head and caressed her rounded baby cheeks. "What shall we do now, my sweet?" Susannah whispered.

The door opened and Evie slipped into the room. She tiptoed to the bed. "Oh! You're awake. I should've known the little one wouldn't wait to be fed."

"Yes, she is most impertinent," Susannah agreed, smiling tenderly at her child. "Thank you for your care, Evie. It was most kind of you to assist me."

With a grin, Evie gave a curtsy. "'Twas the master's orders, mum, but it was a pleasure."

"I must thank your master, also." She invited Evie to sit on the bed, since the maid seemed intent on remaining. They passed a pleasant half hour as the baby took her fill.

Once Cassie's appetite had been sated, Evie said, "The master wants as you should join him for dinner, mum. Will you let me take care of the little one?"

"Oh, no, there's no need—I mean, your master mustn't feel obligated to feed me at his table." Susannah's agitation grew as she thought about facing the tall, handsome gentleman again.

"'Tis his orders, mum," Evie said simply, as if, once uttered, Nicholas Danvers's words were unbreakable.

"You may carry my regrets to your master. What I had earlier will suffice for my dinner."

"Lawsy me, if'n you don't eat more than that, the baby will starve to death."

"Oh, no, truly, Evie, I will be just fine without—"

"My mam would never forgive me if I let you go without a good meal."

Susannah knew the maid was right. She had to keep her strength up if she was to care for her child. "Very well. I'll go down to dinner. But mayn't I take Cassie with me?"

"The master wouldn't like it. I promise I'll take good care of her."

With reluctance Susannah acquiesced to Evie's orders.

"Thank you, Evie, you have been most kind."

The baby had gone back to sleep, tucked warmly under the comforter once again. Evie picked up the hairbrush off the table and stood behind Susannah, brushing her auburn hair to shimmering perfection.

"There is just one thing," Susannah said as she prepared to go downstairs. The urgency in her tone caught Evie's attention. "You must not allow anyone to—to take my baby, whatever story they may tell you. Do you promise me, Evie?"

"Course I do," the maid asserted. "But there be no one who would—"

"No, of course not, but promise me anyway."

"I promise," the maid said and shooed the anxious mama out the door.

Susannah stood poised at the top of the staircase, aware for the first time of the richness of her surroundings. Nicholas Danvers must have a profitable estate. It was certainly much grander than—No. She must completely shut such thoughts away.

As she started down, the squire came out of the library and watched her graceful descent. In spite of the brown wool gown, appropriate wear for a governess, he thought she looked like a princess floating down the stairs. In his mind her beauty was an even greater deterrent to employment than the others she'd presented. With reluctance he moved to the foot of the stairs and held out his arm.

Susannah placed her hand upon the blue superfine-coated arm, her gaze not directly meeting her escort's. "It is most kind of you to invite me to sup with you, sir."

"I will enjoy the company, Miss Brown. It is not often my table is filled with such grace and beauty."

Susannah flashed a questioning glance at her escort's face, not understanding the sudden tightness in his voice, but the smile he gave her seemed pleasant enough and reassuring . . . somewhat.

After they were seated and the first course served,

Susannah expected her host to ask for an explanation of her behavior. However, he led the conversation into general areas, discussing literature, the weather, and even life on a country estate. Without realizing it, Susannah relaxed and responded to his gentle care, talking and eating more than she had in the past month. Even more amazing, she caught herself laughing and enjoying the squire's ridiculous tales of his children's exploits.

"What is it?" she asked when she caught a strange gaze from her host.

"I had not realized dimples must be added to your list of charms, Miss Brown."

Susannah blushed and turned away, the laughter disappearing at once. He sounded more condemning than admiring.

"Shall we take our tea in the parlor?" the squire said abruptly, rising from his chair and offering his arm again.

"I should retire, sir. My baby—"

"Is just fine in Evie's care. She would call if your baby needed you." His features had grown stern, and Susannah's heart thumped in alarm. "And I believe you should explain your behavior this afternoon. After all, you represented yourself as a governess."

2

Before Susannah could answer, Nicholas Danvers led her into a well-proportioned room decorated with old-fashioned furnishings. They were followed immediately by Pritchard and several footmen carrying trays of tea and delicate cakes.

When Pritchard withdrew, Susannah's host nodded for her to serve. An old hand at such duties, she scarce gave a thought to the handling of fragile china, but the squire mentally noted the familiarity. After he had received his tea and declined any cake, he leaned back against the faded gold brocade of the sofa and calmly waited for her to speak.

"I appreciate your hospitality, sir," she said finally, then took a sip of the hot tea. "If I may ask further from you, in the morning, may I be given transportation to the nearest town? Bloomfield, is it? I will board the mail coach there."

"And where will you go?"

The wary look in her eyes was quickly hidden by the dark lashes that swept her rosy cheeks as she stared into her teacup. "To London, of course. I must find another position."

"With a baby accompanying you?"

Susannah set the teacup down and folded her hands in her lap. "Sir, you have been more than generous, and I apologize for taking advantage. If I may be excused?"

The well-mannered gentleman stood as Susannah did, but he reached out to grasp her arm. The warmth of his hand pierced the wool sleeve, and she looked up at him, startled.

"I apologize if I appeared too curious. If you are in difficulties, I am willing to assist you."

Susannah looked away from the sincerity in his warm brown eyes. "Nay, sir, there is no difficulty other than a common one. M-my husband was killed on the Continent, serving his country, and I must support my child and myself." The color rose in her cheeks, and she kept her gaze lowered. However, when he did not release her, she looked up at him.

"Please be seated," he suggested and motioned toward the sofa. Once they were sitting again, he said, "My dear, surely you can see how difficult it will be to find work with a baby in tow."

"I have no choice, sir. I will not abandon my child!" She lifted her head and boldly stared at him.

"And I would never suggest such a thing! But how did you think to assume such a position in the circumstances?"

"I thought I could keep her hidden for a few weeks, until I proved myself adequate to fill the position. Truly, sir, she is a very good baby and would not affect my duties to your children."

He smiled at her naïveté, but something about the young woman tugged at his heart, and he found himself considering her absurd idea. Certainly he could spare one of the staff to assist her with her child while she taught his two rascals. And it would be criminal to send a woman and child out into the world, alone and with no means of support. At least until she had somewhere to go.

"*If* I offered you the position, do you think you could control my boys? They are quite inventive in their approach to schooling."

Hope flashed in her eyes before she carefully banked her enthusiasm. "Sir, I can be firm, and I assure you I will instruct your children well."

"I think I must be insane even to consider such a proposition, but if you are in agreement, I suggest we have one month's trial. If, at the end of that time, you have not fulfilled your position to my satisfaction, or if you are unhappy here with us, then we will end our association." He gave her a considering look, wondering if he was making a mistake. "Is that satisfactory with you?"

"Oh, yes, thank you so much!" Susannah cried, reaching out to touch his hand in gratitude. He curled his warm fingers around hers—to acknowledge their agreement, he told himself.

"I will assign Evie to assist you both with the baby and in the schoolroom, and you must tell me if there is aught you need."

"Of course," she agreed breathlessly, then hesitated. "There—there is one thing."

"Oh?" he said, abruptly pulling his hand free when he realized he'd held on too long to be considered proper.

"I think it best if we keep my baby a secret," she said, her determined gaze pinned to his.

He frowned, surprised by her request. "I don't see how that is possible."

"I don't mean from your staff. I just wondered if you could order them not to—to mention her to others. It might cause talk among your neighbors." She held her breath, awaiting his reply.

"My household is not a hotbed of gossip, but I will mention to Pritchard that it would be best if the child's existence is not bruited about." He watched her curiously. "Will that do?"

"Yes, of course, thank you." Relieved, she stood again. "I will retire now." With a nod from Nicholas, she started to walk away but halted and turned back to him. He raised one eyebrow in question.

"Will Pritchard show me to my room?"

"Are you fearful of losing your way? It is—"

"Oh, no, but the bedchamber I am now using is much too grand for a governess. I realize it cannot be my permanent bedchamber."

"You think you should be housed in the attics?" he asked, a curious smile on his lips.

"I do not expect special privileges, sir," the young woman said, her shoulders back and her head up.

Her dignity impressed him. "You will remain where you are, by my orders." His firm tones left no room for argument, and his eyes dared her to give any dissent.

"Thank you," Susannah murmured, curtsying slightly, and turned to leave.

"Mrs. Brown?"

She turned back again, surprised by his address.

"It is Mrs. Brown, isn't it?"

"Yes, of course." She wished the color in her cheeks would subside.

"Did your husband have no family?"

"No, sir."

"It is amazing that both of you were alone in the world," he murmured, his eyes hooded but trained on her face.

"Perhaps that is what drew us together," she suggested. After dipping another curtsy, she left the room before he could ask any more questions.

Nicholas Danvers stared at the door through which she'd disappeared. He had sworn he would never be swayed by another pretty face. His wife had been a renowned beauty—and had made his life hell. Widowed for two years, he had ignored the attempts of the local matchmakers to lead him into a second marriage. As the wealthiest man in several counties, he was considered an excellent catch. But he would never marry again.

No, he reassured himself, her beauty was not what moved him. It was her absurd courage and inexperience that had caught at his heart. She reminded him of Edward when he tried to stride along in his father's footsteps, his legs too short to reach but his heart refusing to quit.

Ah, well. Time would tell if he'd put too much faith in hoping there was a heart buried beneath her most attractive frame. Still, he was afraid she was too great a beauty to be satisfied for long with a quiet life in the country.

Susannah rose the next morning with hope in her heart for the first time in several months. With Evie's assistance, she breakfasted and tended

to Cassandra's needs before ascending to the
schoolroom.

As she entered, following Evie, she licked her dry
lips nervously. She'd never tried to teach others,
and the home she'd found for herself and Cassie
depended on her ability to do so.

"Morning, Mrs. Colley," Evie sang out as she
entered.

She greeted the elderly woman, who had the
appearance of a grandmother, her gray hair
scraped back in a bun and her face framed by
several chins. Mrs. Colley nodded in return but
said nothing. Seated at the table with her were
Susannah's students.

Edward Danvers slid from his chair and executed
a brief bow as he was presented to the new lady. His
brother, Theodore, followed his example but with a
little less polish.

"I'm very glad to meet all of you," Susannah said,
a warm smile on her face. The two boys responded,
captured by her beauty.

Mrs. Colley only sniffed.

"I wondered if we might visit while the boys
finish their breakfast," Susannah suggested to the
older woman. "Evie will supervise them."

It took several minutes for Susannah to win Mrs.
Colley over. By asking the older woman's advice
and listening to her reminiscences, she reassured
her that her boys would be well cared for. After
almost an hour, they returned to the schoolroom.

Evie breathed a sigh of relief at the acceptance on
Mrs. Colley's face.

Edward and Theodore were a little more appre-
hensive, but they discovered that the lady was as

willing to laugh with them as she was to teach them. When she taught them games and told them a wonderful story about a frog, they were entranced. The final seal to their approval occurred when Evie brought Cassandra to the schoolroom.

Edward extended a finger toward the baby. When a squirming Cassandra wrapped her soft baby fingers around his, he beamed at Susannah. "She likes me!"

"Of course she does," Susannah agreed, smiling. The baby drew her prize to her mouth, and Susannah intervened. "We mustn't let her nibble on your finger, Edward," she said.

The boy giggled, never taking his eyes from the baby.

"I want to see," Theodore said, pushing against his older brother.

"You are too young," Edward said in a superior manner. "A baby must be protected."

Susannah drew the disappointed Theodore into the circle of her arms. "I think Theodore will be careful." Taking his hand, she guided it to the pink skin of the baby's cheek.

"Ooh, she's so soft!" he exclaimed.

Mrs. Colley relaxed. Her babies were safe in this young woman's hands. Even more important, here was a new charge.

By the end of the day the three ladies and the three children were in alt. Nurse Colley cooed over the baby in the nursery, and Susannah and Evie played with the boys.

Nicholas had purposely stayed away from the schoolroom entirely the first day, not wanting

Susannah to think that he was peering over her shoulder. However, as the day went forward, he could think of little else. He feared his generosity to his governess would be injurious to his children. They might easily give their hearts to her only to be devastated when she left.

Though he knew he should avoid continued exposure to a certain pair of blue eyes, he extended an invitation to the new governess to dine at his table that evening. Not only would it ease his servants' burden, but he could also monitor his sons' response to the woman since he included them in the invitation.

Susannah changed into her brown gown, a smile on her lips. Evie, doing up the buttons, congratulated her on her success.

"Thank you, Evie, but I owe you and Mrs. Colley a great deal. I could not have succeeded without your assistance."

"I was that worried over Mrs. Colley. She don't take well to someone else givin' orders to her charges. But you turned her up sweet."

"She was most cooperative, and so good with Cassie. My, in no time, between the two of you, she'll be spoilt," Susannah said with a laugh, showing Evie she was unconcerned.

"Are you sure you don't want her to sleep in the nursery?"

"No, because I must feed her when she awakens. She is too little to be so far from me."

"You should'a had a wet nurse."

"We intended to do so, but the one we'd chosen got very sick the day before I delivered, and there was no one else available. So I nursed Cassie and then—" Susannah looked down at the maid in horror, thinking she had betrayed herself, but Evie was still busy working the buttons on Susannah's gown. "I mean—we couldn't afford one anyway." Evie did up the last button, and Susannah turned around. "How do I look?"

Her hair was drawn back with a yellow bow, its bright color giving life to the dull brown wool. Evie, already under her spell, thought she could not be more beautiful if she had all the crown jewels draped upon her.

Susannah, however, was more critical. Her bosom filled out the dress, but the brown wool hung around her waist, showing the weight loss her difficulties had produced. Smoothing down her skirts, she shrugged off such an unimportant concern.

With a reminder to herself to stay on her guard, she waited in the hall while Evie retrieved the boys and then descended the stairs with a small hand resting in each of hers.

Nicholas heard the excited chatter of his sons from the parlor, where he awaited his guests. One eyebrow slipped up as he realized the young lady had charmed his sons as easily as she might have charmed him in his salad days. Of course, they needed a lady's influence in their lives, and he knew, instinctively, that Mrs. Brown was a lady. But he did not want them to learn at such a young age the bitter lesson his wife had taught him.

Why Mrs. Brown was willing to bury herself in the North of England was a puzzle, as was the reason she'd been brought to the need to support herself. Her story raised more questions than it answered.

However, the squire knew there were many who had fallen from the ranks of society and had to fend for themselves.

The door opened to admit the trio, and Nicholas smiled at the picture they presented, the two boys, dark-haired like their father, on each side of the auburn beauty.

He rose and bowed formally to them. "Good evening. I'm pleased you are joining me."

Edward emulated his father, but little Theodore giggled, covered his face with his free hand, and turned into Susannah's skirt. She bent over and whispered something into the child's ear, and he looked up at her with adoring eyes. With a nod, she curtsied and Theodore bowed, his eyes never leaving his mentor.

Theodore was completely under her spell, his father decided, and probably Edward, also.

Edward said, "Good evening, Father. Thank you for inviting us to join you."

"It is my pleasure," Nicholas replied, a grin on his face, unable to resist his sons' enjoyment.

Theodore looked at Susannah before adding, "Yes, Papa, thank you." Then, with another giggle, he abandoned his newest friend and raced across the room to throw himself at his father.

Susannah watched in fascination. In her mind all day, Nicholas Danvers seemed to be an ideal father, by the servants' talk. But she had been eager to see him with his sons.

Edward followed, receiving his hug, also, but he was much more on his dignity than little Theodore, who saw the proceedings as one of those delightful games Susannah had taught him.

Once seated at the dining table, a son on each side of him and Mrs. Brown beside Theodore, Nicholas asked each of his sons about their first day of instruction.

Their responses flew fast and thick, as each wanted to tell their father of their new discoveries. Susannah watched the man's face out of the corner of her eye, trying to give the impression that she was not concerned.

When the name Cassie appeared in their discourse, he frowned. "Cassie? Who is Cassie?" he asked.

Theodore, a beaming smile on his face, replied, "She's a baby, Papa. A baby girl, and she likes me!"

Nicholas raised an eyebrow and looked at Susannah.

Afraid he would think she had broken their agreement, Susannah explained, "Evie brought my baby up to me in the schoolroom so she could watch the boys while I tended to Cassie. They wanted to see her, and I didn't think it would harm them."

"Of course not," he hastily assured her. "I simply did not recognize the name."

"Her real name is Cassandra," Edward said. "She is very small, Papa. I think she is smaller than Teddy."

"A'course. I'm big!" Theodore protested.

"I meant when you were a baby, silly," Edward explained with a superior smile on his face.

"Oh. Was I great big?" Theodore asked, not sure whether he should be pleased or not.

"Yes, Teddy, you were big," Nicholas said, his mind going back to the difficult delivery from which his wife had never recovered. Something in his face must have concerned Theodore because he looked up at Susannah, alarm in his eyes.

She put her arm about those small shoulders and leaned down to kiss his cheek. "Boys are supposed to be bigger than girls, Teddy, because you must be strong to protect them."

His sunny smile returned and he nodded, squaring his shoulders much in his father's manner. "I will 'tect Cassie," he assured Susannah.

"Thank you, darling."

"Me, too," Edward added, not wanting to be left out.

"That is most kind of you, Master Edward," Susannah said gravely. "Cassandra is a very lucky little girl."

Nicholas said nothing, but he was not displeased. He believed gallantry should be taught at an early age.

"And Susannah told us a frog story," Edward said, catching his father's attention.

"Do you not mean Mrs. Brown?" Nicholas asked sternly. It was the first time either child had so addressed the young woman.

Edward looked first at his father and then at Susannah appealingly. She hurried to respond. "I requested that they address me as Susannah. We are friends, you see."

"Friends or not, Mrs. Brown, my children must maintain good manners. Edward, Theodore, you will address your governess as Mrs. Brown." His stern gaze impressed his children.

"But, Mr. Danvers, surely—"

"Mrs. Brown, there is no room for argument. Proper etiquette must be observed." He turned his attention to the next course that was being served.

For the rest of the meal the children had nothing to say other than monosyllabic answers to their father's questions, and Susannah kept her gaze trained on her plate.

Irritated that his stricture had erased the enthusiasm from his children, Nicholas continued to maintain polite conversation. He would not be defeated by children's sulks or a beautiful young woman's withdrawal.

When the meal finally came to a close, he dismissed the boys to the nursery, giving each a hug before sending them on their way. When Mrs. Brown would've followed them, he asked her to join him in the parlor for tea.

"Thank you, sir, but if you do not mind, I will retire."

"But I do mind, Mrs. Brown," he said smoothly, his eyes shooting off sparks at her refusal.

He gestured for her to precede him into the parlor, and, after a moment's hesitation, Susannah did so.

As the previous evening, Nicholas held his silence while Pritchard directed his minions. Only when the door had closed behind him did Nicholas address the woman sitting stiffly across from him. "I am quite pleased with your efforts today," he said, surprising Susannah.

She had been sure the man had invited her to join him only to reprimand her for her behavior. Still wary, she replied with a quiet, "Thank you."

"Do you think you will have any difficulties with those two?" Affection for his children was evident.

"No, sir, not at all. They are delightful children." The smile on her face matched his.

"Good." He raised his cup in a salute to her success. "Are you happy with the arrangements for your child?"

"Oh, yes. Mrs. Colley has taken Cassie under her wing and will scarce allow anyone else to tend her."

One eyebrow slid up. "Ah, you have charmed Mrs. Colley as well as my children?"

Susannah's cheeks flushed; she was slightly embarrassed, and, unsure whether she'd just been given a compliment or a criticism, she avoided her employer's eyes. "Mrs. Colley is most kind."

Nicholas Danvers studied the governess, his eyes lingering on her soft lips, her delicious figure, until he caught himself fantasizing how it would be to kiss those lips. Startled and irritated by his thoughts, he said briskly, "I wondered if you had need of an advance on your salary. There might be things you need to purchase for you or the child."

Susannah looked up, wide-eyed, wondering if she had offended him with her lack of proper gowns. But his words seemed sincere and kind, even if the tone held little warmth. "Oh, no, thank you, Mr. Danvers, but that is unnecessary."

"But if all your belongings were in the basket you carried, you must have need of something."

"I have a nest egg to provide for the two of us, sir."

"Ah. Well, I will be going into Bloomfield tomorrow if you would care to accompany me and make any purchase necessary." He felt his offer was the least he could do since she had no one else to take her into the town, but it would also give him an opportunity to gauge her reaction to county life.

After all, the shops of Bloomfield were nothing compared to those in York, much less London.

As he waited for her response, her cheeks paled and she shook her head. "No, no, I need nothing."

Frowning, he said, "Perhaps you would like to go along to visit your new surroundings. I would be glad to show you—"

"No, sir, I must remain in the schoolroom," she said, rising even as she spoke. She set down the teacup and hoped the man across from her did not notice her shaking fingers.

Nicholas stood, the frown still on his face, as he watched the young woman beat a hasty retreat, puzzling over the change in her demeanor. Was she frightened of him? Had he, in some fashion, revealed his licentious thoughts? Embarrassed by his own behavior, Nicholas retraced the conversation.

No, her alarm had only arisen when he had mentioned her accompanying him to Bloomfield. But what could there be in Bloomfield that would frighten any young lady, much less one as intrepid as Susannah? A sudden thought occurred to him. Perhaps she was afraid of just being seen.

Not many men would forget such a beauty, he had to admit. If she was hiding for some reason, she could not appear in public without being noted. Perhaps she had run away from her husband, rather than him having died on the Continent.

He had already sensed a secrecy about Susannah, which he detested. His first wife's secrets had been disastrous. Now he felt sure the governess was hiding from someone. Her story was rather vague, and she seemed reluctant to talk about herself, even agitated when the subject came up. Yes, she must be hiding. That could be the only reason for a female to refuse a shopping expedition.

It behooved him to discover what lay behind Susannah's retreat to the country with her baby. After seeing his sons' reaction to the young woman, he wondered again if he might have made a mistake offering her the position. Having given his promise, however, he could not send her away until the end of the month.

He sighed. The days would progress slowly, and he must do all he could to discover her secrets. After all, the sooner her difficulties were resolved, the sooner he would be relieved of the struggle of resisting the auburn beauty.

3

Nicholas strode happily into the schoolroom. "Good morning, Mrs. Brown. How are your students behaving this fine morning?"

"Delightful as always, Mr. Danvers," she assured him, flashing a loving smile to the boys.

"Hmph! I think the gypsies must have stolen Edward and Theodore away and left someone else in their places."

"Papa!" Edward protested. "We've always been good."

Theodore just giggled, having judged rightly that his father was teasing them.

"Well, if that is true, then you should have a reward."

Both boys clamored to know their prize, and Susannah watched them, content in their delight. She'd been their governess for a month now and could not imagine a happier home or family.

She wished as much for Cassandra, but she could not promise her child such happiness. Nor such safety. In the midst of such pleasant surroundings, she had found herself forgetting her difficulties. But she must not.

"I thought I would take you and Mrs. Brown into Bloomfield with me," Nicholas said, interrupting her thoughts. "I have several errands to run, and it is a beautiful day."

Susannah awakened from her thoughts, a frown on her face. Several other times the squire had tried to take her to Bloomfield, but on each occasion she'd found a reason to avoid such an excursion. Did he never give up?

"Thank you, sir, but I must tend to Cassie."

"Nonsense, that is what I pay Mrs. Colley for, is it not? There is no need for you to bury yourself here, Mrs. Brown. I am not a slave driver." He watched her expressive face, wondering what other excuse she would conjure up.

"You are a wonderful employer, sir, but I must decline your kind invitation. Cassie was feverish this morning, and I must remain close. Perhaps another time."

Teddy ran back to lean against Susannah as she sat at the table where they did their lessons. "Cassie is sick?" he said, fear and concern evident in his squeaky voice.

"Not very, darling, but I must stay near her in case she needs me. Do not worry. I'll take good care of her."

Edward looked up at his father and then at Susannah. "We will stay with you if Cassie needs us."

His sacrifice almost brought tears to Susannah's eyes. They were such dear boys. "Thank you, Edward, for your offer, but I believe Cassie will sleep most of the day. But it is a great comfort to know that you and Theodore are willing to help."

Nicholas Danvers appreciated his governess's response. Some adults might have scorned Edward's offer. But she took special care to consider their tender feelings. His children's adoration of Mrs. Brown reassured him. In spite of his concern about the future, he could not fault her performance the past month. He had intended to send her on her way, but she had become such a part of his household, he could not do so now without his entire staff thinking him a monster.

Gathering his sons, Nicholas left the schoolroom. Too much lately his thoughts had been focused on Mrs. Brown, but he was no closer now to discovering her secret than he had been that first night. Each evening she dined with him, but their conversation remained impersonal or dealt with his children. He found she was quite skillful at avoiding any questions. And any excursions to Bloomfield.

He *had* discovered, though, that she was warmhearted, loved children, dealt kindly with his servants, and was much appreciated by them. However, she had not left his home once since her arrival, no matter how many times he had offered to escort her.

His wife, Elinor, had complained bitterly about the quiet country life and the dearth of decent shopping. His own sisters had even commented often about the distance from any good shops. But Mrs. Brown seemed quite content never to set foot in a shop again.

Her reclusiveness and secrecy frustrated him. He knew there was a reason for her sequestering herself on his estate and seeing no one, and he was

anxious to discover it. He also wondered how long
she would stay. His children would be very upset
when she left, but he would be relieved. Resisting
her beauty and charm, a path to which he was committed, took a great deal of energy.

"Papa, will you buy us a sticky bun at the inn?"
Edward asked, bringing his parent back to his present situation.

"Yes, son, if you are on your best behavior." He
decided to put aside his worries and enjoy the day
with his children. However, he might just ask if there
had been any inquiries in town about his governess.

With her charges taken away, Susannah could not
fill her day with stories or games, so she sought
out Pritchard for other duties. Lately, he had been
bringing domestic problems to her for advice, most
particularly the choice of new draperies in the parlor, as the squire had decided the old ones needed
replacing.

Pritchard, while willing to do anything for his
employer, felt inadequate in choosing colors. When
he hesitantly asked for Susannah's assistance, she
had been delighted. She loved choosing furnishings
and felt she had a talent for picking appealing colors
and patterns.

Even more important, in Pritchard's mind,
Susannah had offered several new recipes to Cook,
adding variation to their meals and improving the
overall preparation.

Today, Pritchard and his underlings were hanging the new draperies, and she entered the parlor to
watch. The two of them were discussing their handi-
work when a footman came into the room.

"Mr. Pritchard, Lady Arbor be here."

Pritchard rushed from the room, leaving Susannah wondering who Lady Arbor could be. Immediately he showed in a woman of medium height, her dark hair arranged elegantly under her bonnet, which topped a fashionable ruby-red merino gown.

"Lady Arbor, this is Mrs. Brown, the new governess. Mrs. Brown, may I present Lady Jane Arbor, the master's sister," Pritchard said hurriedly.

"Good morning. I understand my brother is from home," the lady said pleasantly, her voice cool.

"Yes, my lady," Susannah replied. "He took his children to Bloomfield to run some errands."

"How fortunate for you," the woman said even as she turned to look at the new draperies.

Susannah resented the implication that she would prefer not to perform her duties, but she said nothing in return. After a moment she suggested to Pritchard, "Perhaps Lady Arbor would like a tea tray, Pritchard. I'll clear out the others so she may sup in peace."

The lady turned and stared at Susannah. "How thoughtful of you, my dear. Yes, Pritchard, I would enjoy some tea, and some of Cook's fare. Has she finally learned to make cakes?"

"Yes, my lady. Mrs. Brown gave her some very good recipes."

"Ah, a woman of many talents."

Susannah caught the woman's less than complimentary meaning, but Pritchard took her words at face value. "Yes, my lady. She also chose the draperies we are hanging. She has been of great assistance."

"How helpful of you, Mrs. Brown."

"Thank you, my lady," Susannah murmured as she turned away.

"Oh, Mrs. Brown, don't leave, please. I'd appreciate your company while I take my tea."

The woman looked anything but pleased, and Susannah wondered why she had issued the invitation. However, Susannah had no choice once the words were spoken. "Of course, my lady." She nodded at Pritchard and sat down across from Nicholas's sister.

When tea had been served and all the servants had withdrawn, Lady Arbor leaned back among the cushions and stared at Susannah. "And how do you enjoy my nephews?"

"They are very sweet."

"I remember them as little imps."

"They can be mischievous, of course, but I find them most cooperative." Susannah sipped her tea and waited for the next question.

"And my brother?"

Susannah blinked. She had expected questions concerning her qualifications. "I beg your pardon?"

"Do you find my brother sweet, also?"

"My lady, I do not understand your question."

The woman stared down her nose at her, and Susannah wished she could retire to the schoolroom. "It is a simple question."

"Your brother is a kind employer."

Her stiff words did not appear to satisfy Lady Arbor. "Yes, so I've heard. But—"

"Jane! What are you doing here?" At that moment Nicholas Danvers entered the room, excited and happy to see his sister. Trailing behind him were both boys, who went immediately to Susannah to tell her of their outing.

Instead of answering her brother, the lady eyed the children. "What? Do I get no greeting from my nephews?"

Both boys grinned and left Susannah's side to hug their aunt. It was the first time Susannah warmed to the guest. If Teddy and Edward liked her, then she must have redeeming qualities.

"And you have not answered my question. Has Peter tired of your incessant badgering?" Nicholas teased.

"Nick! You know I do not—Oh, you are such a tease! Of course not. He went to London on business, and I took advantage of his absence to pay my brother a visit. Is that satisfactory?"

Susannah would've groaned if she'd been alone. The woman would be staying. Her peaceful world had been invaded.

"Of course it is. We are delighted to have you," Nicholas assured her.

"Good. I had my bags taken up to my old room," Lady Arbor said in an offhand manner.

The silence that greeted her remark warned Susannah of the squire's response. "Sorry, old girl, but Mrs. Brown is occupying that room. But I'm sure Pritchard has found a place for you."

"I will be happy to remove to another chamber," Susannah said at once, not wanting to make the situation any more uncomfortable.

With a flinty look above her smile, Lady Arbor murmured, "Of course not. I could not put you to so much trouble."

Nicholas rushed in. "That is not necessary, Mrs. Brown. There are several other chambers more spacious than yours. Jane will be quite comfortable."

"Very well," Susannah said. "Shall I take the boys upstairs now, sir?" She hoped their presence would provide her with an excuse to leave.

"Yes, of course. They ate lunch at the inn, however, so don't think I have starved them."

"But, Papa, that was hours ago," Edward protested, even as he willingly reached for Susannah's hand. Theodore, already clinging to Susannah, grinned but said nothing.

"I think Cook saved you a snack just in case you returned hungry," she assured them as she led them away.

Nicholas's gaze followed the governess and his children from the room. His sister said nothing until he once again noticed her presence.

"A governess, Nick?"

"Mrs. Brown? Yes, of course, she is the governess. What do you mean?" Surprised by his sister's question, he turned to stare at her.

"I mean she is much too beautiful to fill such a position." She looked pointedly at her brother. "And you seem much too interested in your governess."

Nicholas frowned at his sister. "I don't take your meaning, Jane."

She set her teacup down on the table beside the sofa. "I came to visit because I received a disturbing letter from Mrs. Dilby."

"That tattlemonger? What story is she telling now?" Nicholas relaxed, since he knew he had done nothing to stir the local gossips. Any improper thoughts he had had remained only in his head.

"Nick, she told me that you had refused all invitations the past month." Jane chewed on her bottom lip before she added, "And she is talking about a baby."

Nicholas's features stiffened, and one eyebrow rose in challenge. "And?"

"Is that not enough?"

"No. I can deny neither of those things. However, they are unrelated, and neither is cause for concern."

"Who's baby is it?"

"Mrs. Brown's. Her name is Cassandra, and she is, um, two months old."

"And the father?" Jane asked, her anxious eyes focused on her brother's face.

"Mr. Brown, I presume." He looked at his sister, astounded. "Did you really think I had brought my bastard to live here with Edward and Theodore?"

"I know you to be a loving and kind person, Nick. I don't think you would abandon a child just because you were not married to the mother."

Calmly he took his sister's hands in his. "No, I would not, love, but I swear to you I had never seen Mrs. Brown before she appeared on my doorstep one month ago, sent by the agency I had contacted in London."

"She arrived with a baby? And you hired her?"

Nicholas smiled ruefully. "I know. It sounds preposterous, doesn't it? I considered it so myself. But you've met her. She is beautiful, of course, but that is not the reason I hired her. You, of all people, should know I would not succumb to beauty. I admired her courage, and I was fearful for her innocence." He rose and took a few steps before facing his sister. "And I have been well rewarded.

She is an excellent governess. Edward and Theodore love her."

"And the baby?"

"Ah. Surprisingly, the baby was an added benefit. She gives Colley something to do, so she does not mind sharing my two with Mrs. Brown." Nicholas laughed at the thought of the way Mrs. Colley hovered over Cassandra.

"So why have you refused all invitations?"

Nicholas shrugged. "There have not been that many. After all, this area is not a hotbed of social events." He grinned at his sister before continuing. "There is much to occupy my time. Besides, you know every party I attend I have to ward off the matchmaking mamas. I grow weary of it."

Jane moved to her brother's side. "Dearest, I know your marriage with Elinor was not ... not a happy one, but don't you think you should consider remarriage?"

Nicholas showed no hesitation in his response. "No, we are fine just as we are."

"Edward and Theodore need a mother."

"Nonsense. They are happy, as am I."

Jane sighed. She knew how stubborn her brother could be. She would just have to find more subtle ways to persuade him to alter his life. Standing on tiptoe, Jane kissed her only brother on his cheek. "Very well. But I hope you will venture out occasionally with me. I want to see all my old friends while I am here."

Nicholas groaned in protest but did not refuse to accompany her, and Jane considered herself the winner. "I shall now go discover the chamber Pritchard has chosen for me and supervise my unpacking. I'll see you at dinner."

"Before you go," Nicholas said, halting her before she opened the door, "there is one thing I would have you do for me while you are here."

"What is that, dear brother? Teach Cook how to prepare better meals?"

"No, Mrs. Brown has done that," he murmured without thinking. His mind was concentrating on how to phrase his request. "Mrs. Brown is most . . . secretive about her past."

Jane's eyebrows rose, but she said nothing.

"I am not being a nosyparker, but I believe she is in some difficulty, which would explain her burying herself in the country. I will not turn her out. She has done an exemplary job of taming my imps. But the longer she remains, the more attached the boys will become. I want to resolve her difficulties so the break will come before it will do much damage. However, she has not trusted me with her problem. I thought, since you are a woman, she might be more willing to talk to you."

"What makes you think she is hiding something?"

Nicholas clasped his hands behind his back and paced across the room. "She avoids all personal conversation. I know as little about her past now as I did when she first arrived."

"Perhaps she isn't aware of your interest. After all, I'm sure you've seldom had opportunity for casual conversation."

"We dine together every evening." Irritated by his sister's rationale, Nicholas did not notice how her gaze sharpened at his words. "But it is more than that. She has not left the house since she arrived."

"You mean she never goes out for a breath of fresh air?"

"No, of course not. She takes the boys outside frequently." He cleared his throat. "I have offered to escort her to Bloomfield to make any purchases she might need, but she has refused."

"So she needs nothing," Jane said, shrugging.

"Jane, she arrived with only a wicker basket. She has two dresses to her name, and Cassie has little more."

"Nicholas," Jane said, walking back across the room to him, "that is not unusual for someone in her lowly position. Perhaps she cannot afford more clothes." Jane, who loved beautiful gowns, felt a stirring of sympathy for the young woman.

"I offered her an advance on her salary, but she refused that, also. She would not even accompany me and the boys today, just for an outing."

"Perhaps she is shy, or reclusive, or . . . it could be that she *is* aware of your interest," Jane suggested boldly.

"What *are* you talking about?"

"Oh, Nick, it is so obvious that you are attracted to her. It could be that she is trying to avoid a slip on the shoulder."

"I am going to have a talk with Peter about your language, young lady," Nicholas growled. "Besides, I would never offer an affair to someone like Mrs. Brown. She is a lady, whatever position she may occupy."

"Nick! Surely you wouldn't marry a—a governess!"

"There is no reason why I should not. I am not a peer of the realm even if my sister is married to one.

I am a plain country squire, Jane, no more and no less."

"You are the best catch between here and London, and you know it! Surely you—"

"Enough! I am not proposing marriage to Mrs. Brown. I would never marry for beauty again, even were I to consider marriage, which I am not. I just want to know if she is in trouble. Will you try to be a friend to her, Jane? Please?"

Jane had never been able to refuse her brother anything when he pleaded with her. "Very well. But if I uncover something sordid, you must promise me you will not get involved."

"I have no intention of becoming involved," he assured her with distaste. "I simply want to protect my children."

With a sigh, Jane gave up the argument. "I really must retire, brother dear. I will befriend your Mrs. Brown, but it must wait until after I've had a laydown. I don't remember traveling being so tiring."

Nicholas studied her. "You do look pale, Jane. I'll have Pritchard escort you to your chamber. Rest until dinner."

Jane only smiled wearily in response as Nicholas led her out to the entry hall and summoned Pritchard. She really was exhausted. And her brother had given her a lot to think about.

After spending several more hours with Teddy and Edward, Susannah retrieved Cassie from the nursery and descended to her bedchamber. Lady Arbor's bedchamber. The woman had not been pleased to find her in residence, much less in her very own bedchamber.

Ah, well, there was no help for it. His sister's presence meant, of course, that Nicholas would not expect her to come down to dinner. The change would be both a relief and a disappointment. She enjoyed the companionship she shared with her employer, but she also realized she was coming to depend on him too much in spite of his reserve. He never relaxed with her as he did with his sons. But then, neither did she, always keeping her thoughts to herself. She could not afford to reveal her secrets.

Her future was so unsure. She'd thought that if she could find a safe place for a few months, she would be able to determine what she should do. She was still secretly hoping something would happen to Gerald, and then felt guilty for even thinking such a thing.

Her last resort would be to emigrate to America. But would she be safe, even there? She cuddled her child tightly against her until Cassandra protested. Susannah stared down into the bright little face, her eyes blue like her mother's. Because of Cassie, she must not give up. Her daughter deserved to take her rightful place in the world.

Sighing, Susannah placed Cassie in the crib the footman had brought to her room. There was no need to change to that revolting gown she'd worn each evening since her arrival. She thought of the beautiful silk and lace gowns hanging in her wardrobe at home. No, she must never allow herself to think of the past. She must fight for her future, hers and Cassie's.

4

As the clock struck six, Evie slipped into Susannah's chamber. "The master wants to know should he set back dinner?"

Susannah, propped up comfortably against her pillows on the bed, looked up from her book in surprise. Earlier she'd collected one of her favorite stories from the library to read while she dined in her room.

"But I thought he would want to dine alone with his sister."

"The two of them are waitin' in the parlor for you to join them," Evie assured her.

"Oh, dear!" Susannah exclaimed as she slid quickly from the bed. Whisking off the wrapper she'd put on earlier, she reached for the usual brown gown. "Help me, please, Evie," she requested hurriedly, turning her back for the maid to fix the buttons for her.

"Shall I do your hair?" Evie asked, her nimble fingers finishing her chore.

"There is no time. Just wind the braid in a circle at

the nape of my neck. I doubt Mr. Danvers nor Lady Arbor will notice."

As soon as Evie had inserted pins to hold her hair in place, Susannah scooted down the stairs to arrive at the parlor door, breathless.

"My apologies, Mr. Danvers."

"Not at all, Mrs. Brown. I was only concerned whether you needed more time." She felt his gaze rove over her toilette, and her cheeks flushed.

"No, thank you, sir, I am ready to dine."

"Very well. Shall we, Jane?" he asked, extending an arm to his sister, who rose from the sofa, her blue silken skirt fluttering down around her.

Susannah bit her lip as a longing for graceful clothing filled her. She swallowed her jealousy and turned to follow her host and his sister. As he came even with her, however, he extended his other arm.

"Mrs. Brown?"

She should not have been surprised at his courtesy. He had ever treated her as a guest, not an employee. Lightly placing her hand on his sleeve, she walked alongside the other two to the dining room.

Lady Jane Arbor had paid special attention when Mrs. Brown raced into the parlor. Despite her brother's assurance that Susannah was only the governess, she had her doubts. Now, after her brother had offered his other arm to Susannah, they walked three abreast to the dining room. Pritchard held out her chair for her, and Lady Arbor sat down across from Susannah, with her brother seated between them at the head of the table.

After the servants had served the first course, she

took several sips of the turtle soup before saying, "I understand you are from London, Mrs. Brown. How do you enjoy the country?"

Though there was a barely perceptible pause in Mrs. Brown's response, she said simply, "Very well, my lady, thank you."

"But surely you miss the shops, the entertainment?" Lady Arbor persisted, mindful of her brother's request that she extract information from the governess.

"No, my lady. Do you enjoy the theater?"

"Well, it is diverting, of course, but the most enjoyment is to be had from watching those in attendance. The last time we visited the theater, there was the most amusing—" Jane broke off abruptly when she noticed the exasperation on her brother's face. Turning back to Susannah, she said, "That is, do you enjoy the theater, Mrs. Brown?"

"I have only been in attendance once, my lady. Did you ever see the great Edmund Kean perform?"

"Oh, yes, several times, though the last was rather sad. I'm afraid he took the stage slightly the worse for his indulgence and almost fell into the pit several times. He was playing the role of Hamlet, but the audience roared with laughter as he staggered his way through the part." Jane laughed at the memory.

Pritchard brought in the next course, curried salmon, and the diners prepared to taste Cook's newest offering.

"Cook has certainly improved her dishes, Pritchard," Lady Arbor said to the butler. "Please send her my compliments."

"Thank you, my lady. She will be greatly pleased by your commendation." The butler nodded at

Susannah as he left the room, a fact noted by Lady Arbor.

"I understand you have brought about the change, Mrs. Brown." She watched the other woman's cheeks flush.

"I simply offered some recipes my aunt had given me."

Nicholas nodded before saying, "You also instigated a cleanliness in the kitchen to which Cook had never abscribed before, Mrs. Brown. I don't think I have expressed my appreciation for your efforts before now, but please believe they have been enjoyed."

The young lady murmured thank you and nodded before eating her salmon, making no attempt to capitalize on her employer's attention or draw further compliments from him. Lady Arbor watched her intently. Could she be as modest as she appeared? Or was she playing a part in front of company?

"Do you cook yourself, Mrs. Brown?"

Her brother's quick frown told Jane he didn't think her question appropriate, since ladies of quality were not inclined to visit the kitchens, but she waited for an answer.

Calmly Susannah wiped her lips on the napkin and said, "My aunt—that is, I was raised to believe one should know how to provide for oneself, whatever one's station in life." She lifted her blue-eyed gaze to Lady Arbor as if in challenge.

"A very good philosophy. You were raised by your aunt?"

After a slight hesitation Susannah said, "Yes, my lady."

"What happened to your parents?"

"Jane, I believe you had best eat your salmon before Pritchard returns to carry it away, or Cook will not believe your compliments to be sincere," Nicholas said, intervening in her inquisition. He began to think it had not been such a good idea to have Jane try and draw out Susannah. She had not been very delicate or discreet in her questioning.

A quick look at her brother's face and Jane decided to give up her role of investigator this evening. She didn't understand Nicholas tonight. It seemed her efforts had not pleased him.

Nicholas finished the second course in silence, as did his female companions. His sister's clumsy attempts to extract information from Susannah had embarrassed him and probably made the lovely woman beside him nervous and uncomfortable.

After a side of beef was served, along with potatoes, he turned to his sister. "Jane, if you care to ride on the morrow, your favorite mount is available."

"Oh, Snowball is still here? I'm so pleased! Yes, I'll ride first thing in the morning. Shall you join me?" Her face was lit with pleasure, and she watched her brother for his answer.

"No, my dear, I cannot in the morning. Perhaps Mrs. Brown would care to ride with you. There is another lady's mount in the stables, Mrs. Brown."

The flash of pleasure in her dazzling blue eyes rocked him as he watched her, but it died out almost at once. Her gaze dropped to her plate, and she said sedately, "Thank you, Mr. Danvers, but I do not have a riding habit with me."

He studied her as she reached for a drink of water,

noticing the slight trembling of her fingers.

"But you do ride?"

"I—I have ridden on occasion in the past, sir, but not lately."

He picked up his knife and fork and appeared to concentrate on the meat on his plate, but he said sternly, "You must go to Bloomfield and order a riding habit to be made for you, Mrs. Brown, at my expense, of course. My sons will want to be in the saddle now that the weather has begun to warm, and I will expect you to accompany them."

"But I cannot—that is, I cannot leave Cassie alone."

Thoroughly chewing the meat he'd just placed in his mouth, Nicholas watched her, her gaze meeting his and then falling rapidly to the plate in front of her, where her portion of meat remained untouched.

"Is Cassie the—I mean, is Cassie your baby?" Jane asked, her eyes curious.

"Yes. Your brother was most kind to hire me in the circumstances, my lady, and I do try not to let my child interfere in my duties, but—"

"We both know Mrs. Colley would protest if you shortened her time with Cassandra," Nicholas said, interrupting her speech. "There is no reason for you not to attend the boys when they ride."

"Surely they will need to receive instruction. I'm sure you have someone in the stables more capable of providing such instruction than I, sir."

Blue eyes pleaded with him for understanding, but he hardened his heart against them. "You will do as I say, Mrs. Brown. Even if it means going into Bloomfield." He added the last in measured words, watching her face. Her eyes widened with what he was tempted to call fear before she shuttered them with her thick lashes.

"La, there is no need to go into Bloomfield," Jane said with a laugh. "Mrs. Hardy will come to you, Mrs. Brown, in the wink of an eye. She always did so for my sister and me, and I'm sure she did for Elinor, when she ever deigned to order anything, which she always swore was outmoded. Just write her a note in the morning, and she'll be here before luncheon."

Nicholas stared angrily at Jane, and too late she realized her mistake. He'd finally had Susannah forced into going to Bloomfield before his beloved chatterbox of a sister ruined it.

Susannah, on the other hand, was delighted. "Thank you, Lady Arbor. That is an excellent idea. I hate to give up my time in the schoolroom. You do not mind if I follow Lady Arbor's suggestion, Mr. Danvers?"

Nicholas fumed beneath his grim smile. "Of course not, Mrs. Brown. Whatever is most convenient for you."

An awkward silence fell between them before Jane thought of a way to appease her brother. "I have it! I brought two riding habits with me, Mrs. Brown. While my second habit is not in the latest mode, and might not fit you perfectly, you would be decently clad. Why not use it so you may join me for a ride in the morning?"

Nicholas watched his governess flash a questioning glance his way before she turned to his sister. "If you would not mind, my lady, I would be delighted to join you. That is, if you intend to ride before breakfast. I must not be tardy to the schoolroom."

"I would enjoy your company, my dear, since my brother has refused me," Jane replied, a teasing look at her brother. "I must warn you, Nick. There is an old saying about all work and no play. You should heed my words."

"Oh, I shall, sister dear, I shall."

The royal blue velvet riding habit that Lady Arbor felt was sadly *démodé* was the most stylish garment Susannah had donned in months. She pirouetted before the cheval glass, enjoying the feel of expensive clothing.

Even boots had been discovered in the attic. The former mistress of the manor house had scarcely worn them before her death. All that was needed was some cloth to stuff in the toes.

Added to the stylish garments were cheeks flushed with excitement at the prospect of a ride and sparkling blue eyes.

When Susannah tripped down the stairs at an early hour, the matching hat tipped rakishly over her auburn curls, Pritchard informed her that Lady Arbor was taking an early cup of tea in the breakfast parlor.

"Good morning," Susannah said brightly to her riding companion, who did not appear at all well. As Susannah took in her appearance, she asked, "Are you ill, my lady?"

"I did not think it would be so obvious." Jane closed her eyes briefly before raising the steaming cup of tea to her lips. When she'd taken a reviving drink, she added, "I think I congratulated Cook too soon last evening. The curried salmon seems to have upset me."

"I am so sorry, my lady. I hope Mr. Danvers did not also suffer ill effects." Susannah studied the woman slumped in her seat. "Perhaps some toasted bread would ease your discomfort."

Jane moaned. "Even the thought of food makes me ill. No, I will just have my tea."

"Are you sure you feel up to riding this morning, my lady?" Though she felt compelled to offer the sacrifice of giving up her ride, Susannah held her breath, hoping it would not be necessary.

"No, no, a ride will make me feel better." Lady Arbor picked up her cup and drained it. "There, I am ready." She stood, but then noticed her companion had not yet finished her tea. "Oh, I am sorry. Do you want—"

But Susannah had already risen. "No, I am ready. I'm truly looking forward to riding again. I cannot thank you enough for loaning me your habit."

"It looks very good on you. Perhaps you should ask Mrs. Hardy to copy the color for your new habit."

The two ladies walked through the house to the door leading to the stableyard. Susannah pulled it open, and the invigoratingly crisp spring air rushed in to meet them. Susannah's eyes fluttered closed as she drew a deep breath filled with anticipation. But Jane shuddered.

"I have grown soft since my marriage and consequent move to the south. It is considerably warmer on our estate."

"You will soon readjust, my lady," Susannah assured, not wanting anything to dim the beauty of the morning.

The head groomsman had their mounts saddled

and waiting in the stableyard. However, he was not alone. Standing beside him, the reins to a strong bay stallion in his hands, was Nicholas Danvers.

"I thought you were too occupied to accompany us this morning?" Jane demanded when she saw him.

Nicholas watched the two ladies approach, drawing in a sharp breath when he had a clear picture of his governess. He had never seen her dressed before in anything that showed her to advantage. The royal blue of the habit lit up her eyes, and its snug fit revealed slender curves hidden by her shapeless gowns. Her beauty took his breath away, causing panic to rise within him. He had promised himself he would never again be swayed by such a thing. Consequently, his response to his sister was somewhat brusque.

"I changed my mind."

"Shall I return to the house, then?" Mrs. Brown questioned. Although she'd be disappointed, she still hoped she could ride later that day or the next morning.

"No!" He recovered his composure and added, "I changed my plans because I wanted to be sure you were comfortable with your mount, Mrs. Brown. I don't want to send you out with my children if you are not competent in the saddle."

"Well, really, Nick, have you no concern for me?" Jane asked jokingly, pulling her brother's attention from his governess to her.

"Why would I, you repellent brat?" he teased, relaxing once more. "You have been in the saddle since you were Teddy's age. In fact, several times you made my life most difficult because of your escapades on horseback."

Jane smiled at Susannah. "Brothers never forget. Do you have any brothers?"

Susannah, who had been making friends with the black beauty she was to ride, continued to rub the mare's nose, answering offhandedly, "No, I have no brothers or sisters."

Nicholas ignored his sister's triumphant grin. He already knew Mrs. Brown had no family. "Shall we mount up?" he suggested. He motioned for his groomsman to assist his sister, and he offered a hand to Susannah. Her swift ascent to the saddle and calm demeanor demonstrated her skills.

After he mounted his bay, the three riders headed across the west pasture. He hung back a little and watched the two ladies ahead of him. As competent a rider as his sister was, Susannah outshone her. She rode as easily as if she were sitting on a sofa in the drawing room.

"Where are we going?" Jane asked, looking back at Nicholas for guidance.

"I thought we would ride over to Mrs. Scott's. Her youngest has been ill." Much to his surprise, Susannah turned around.

"But that is Evie's name."

"Yes, she is Evie's mother."

Little else was said until their arrival at the thatched cottage where the widow Scott resided with her children. Nicholas dismounted but suggested the two women remain on top their horses. "There is no need for you to expose yourselves to the sickness when we do not know what it might be."

"If you please, Mr. Danvers, may I accompany you? I would like to be able to report back to Evie about the child's condition." Susannah was worried and felt this was the least she could do for the maid, who had also become her friend.

Nicholas looked up into her concerned face, surprised. His servants had grown fond of the woman, but he now understood why. "Very well." Reaching up strong hands, he clasped her small waist and lifted her down from her mount.

Jane said, "I refuse to be left here. I'll come, too."

"My lady, we shall only be a minute, and you were not feeling well this morning. I do not think it would be wise to risk more sickness."

Jane's face reflected the discomfort she'd experienced earlier that morning as she considered Susannah's words. "Perhaps you are right. But do not be too long."

After a knock, Nicholas opened the door in response to a voice inviting them in and gestured for Susannah to precede him. They entered a room that was scrupulously clean, though sparsely furnished. By the fireplace a gray-haired woman was bent over a makeshift bed, where a small form lay motionless.

Looking over her shoulder, she straightened up at once when she recognized one of her guests. "Mr. Danvers, sir! I didn't know it be you. Welcome." She bustled over to him, wiping her hands on her apron.

"Good morning, Mrs. Scott. How is little Jamie?"

"It's that kind of you to ask, sir. He be better this morning. The fever broke late last night." Though she answered the squire, her eyes were fixed on the lady beside him.

"My apologies, Mrs. Scott. I should have presented Mrs. Brown at once."

He watched as Susannah extended her hand to Mrs. Scott before saying quietly, "I'm pleased to hear your child is better. I'll be sure to tell Evie."

"You be the Mrs. Brown Evie helps at the big house?"

"Yes, Mrs. Scott, and Evie is such a wonderful child. She is a marvelous help to me."

The lady's tired face lit up with pleasure. "Oh, ma'am, she's a right good child, she is. I do miss her, but she comes over most every day and helps me when she can."

"I'll try to see she gets a little extra time while her brother is ill, Mrs. Scott." She paused to look up at her employer. "That is, if Mr. Danvers does not object."

"No, of course not." A stirring from the bed drew everyone's attention. "We'll not keep you from Jamie's side, Mrs. Scott. I just wanted to be sure you have everything you need. The doctor has been to call?"

"Yes, sir, he came yesterday. Thank you for your kindness."

He took the lady's hand and patted it. "Nonsense. Your John died fighting for our country. It is the least I can do."

Taking Susannah by the elbow, he escorted her from the cottage after saying their goodbyes. Before he assisted her to mount, he said, "When Evie comes today, tell Pritchard to have Cook fix a basket of food. It will save Mrs. Scott some effort, preparing for her family."

"Yes, sir," Susannah said, her eyes on his face. As he reached out to settle his hands around her waist once more, she said, "You are a very good man, Mr. Danvers."

Her solemn beauty, her nearness, the warmth of her body beneath his hands, all brought a longing so forceful he wanted to forget his past and take what would assuage the desire her beauty aroused. Pushing his unwanted thoughts away, he sedately settled her back in the saddle and said, "Not as good as I should be, Mrs. Brown, I can assure you." With a wry smile on his lips, he turned to mount his own horse and answer the questions his sister was already asking about their visit.

5

After their ride the threesome ate breakfast together. Lady Arbor appeared to have recovered from her earlier infirmity, eating and talking with equal fervor.

"La, I don't know when I've had such an appetite. I must have a care or my clothing will not fit. This habit is feeling quite snug, and I only had it made two months ago."

Nicholas scarcely acknowledged his sister's remarks. Ever since they'd left Mrs. Scott's cottage, he'd been withdrawn. Susannah thought his preoccupation with his people an admirable trait.

"I am glad you also have a healthy appetite, Mrs. Brown," Jane continued. "It makes me feel less greedy."

"Mrs. Brown does not eat enough," Nicholas muttered, as if speaking to himself. Susannah was slightly annoyed by his comment, and she began to feel self-conscious as his gaze roved over her form.

"At least I am not a scarecrow, as I was when I first arrived," she reminded him with a tight smile. His answering smile, however, made her heart race unexpectedly. He was such a charming man when he chose to be.

"Had you been ill?" Jane asked.

Susannah's eyes shifted from her employer to her plate.

"No, but I had just given birth to my baby."

"My friend, Lady Crosby, gave birth last year, but she did not grow any smaller as a result." Jane paused to take another bite. "My husband and I hope to have a family. My sister already has three children. . . ." She trailed off with a look of longing on her face.

Even her brother noticed her sad face and reached over to pat her hand. "All in good time, Jane. Enjoy your life together. Once you start a family, you'll find yourself much more occupied."

She sighed. "I suppose you are right, but I am sure I am older than Mrs. Brown, and she already has a child." Though good manners forbade her asking Susannah her age, she asked, "How long were you married, Mrs. Brown?"

"Almost two years," Susannah said, though in truth her marriage had lasted only a little over a year, ending with her husband's death while she was *enceinte*.

"We have been married for five years."

"At least your marriage is a happy one," Nicholas reminded her in an attempt to raise her spirits.

It was Jane's turn to offer comfort. "I know. And I am sorry your marriage was so disastrous. I never thought Elinor would—"

"Thank you, love," Nicholas said hurriedly, his face flushed, interrupting his sister, "but it is best forgotten."

Jane looked as if she wanted to say something else, but the expression on her brother's face stopped her. She turned her attention to Susannah.

"It is sad that your happy marriage ended so tragically, Mrs. Brown."

Susannah murmured a quiet thank you but said nothing else.

"I do not believe Mrs. Brown said her marriage was a happy one," Nicholas commented, surprising his companions.

"Nick," Jane protested, her eyes wide, "that is most—"

"My apologies, Mrs. Brown."

Susannah nodded in acknowledgment of his words but avoided his gaze. Before anything else could be said, Pritchard entered the room.

"Mrs. Brown, Mrs. Hardy is here to see you."

Susannah stood up with relief. She did not want to discuss her marriage with anyone, especially her employer. "Thank you, Pritchard. I will come at once."

Once the governess had exited the room, Jane turned to her brother once more. "I am sorry I brought up your marriage in front of Mrs. Brown. It is just that you deserve happiness. That is why I think you should remarry, Nick. I want you to have the happiness I share with Peter," Jane said, leaning toward her brother.

"My dear, I am perfectly happy as I am."

"Are there no delightful young women in the country? Surely there are several ladies who would take on you along with Theodore and Edward?"

"There are any number of women who have shown themselves available, my dear Jane, and, if I may shock you, they have not all been concerned with marriage vows," he explained with exasperation.

"But, Nick—"

"No, Jane, you must promise to abandon any matchmaking plans. I have no desire to remarry."

Jane fell silent, saddened by her brother's attitude. Suddenly she felt inexplicably exhausted. "I believe I will retire to my chamber for a rest. The ride tired me more than I thought."

She excused herself, leaving her brother staring moodily across the room.

Women! His sister would not leave him alone, determined to return him to the married state. Susannah's presence was also bothering him. Though she did not do so intentionally, he found her beauty devastating to his determination to avoid all women like his wife.

When he clasped her small waist to lift her to her horse, a desire he had not experienced since before his marriage had flooded him. He vowed again to avoid touching the woman. Unfortunately, his hands were more easily controlled than his thoughts. They continued to dwell on the lovely governess long after she had left his presence.

Susannah couldn't hide her enthusiasm at the prospect of a new riding habit. She even decided to splurge and purchase a new gown to wear to dinner in the evenings. The hated brown wool would not have to be worn every evening. Though she wanted to make additional purchases, she refrained. With Cassandra and her future so unsettled, she could not do so.

It was tempting to feel safe, secure, here in Mr. Danvers's home. But in her heart, Susannah knew Gerald would search until he found her. She had gained a respite from the danger, but it would arise again. She and Cassandra would have to find another hiding place. But not yet. Not yet.

After her meeting with the seamstress, Susannah ascended to the schoolroom and dismissed Evie to go to her mother's cottage. "And stop by the kitchen, Evie. I asked Pritchard to have Cook prepare some special food for your mother."

When Evie would have protested, she added, "I am doing so on the squire's orders."

Tears shone in the maid's eyes. "You both be so kind."

Susannah patted her shoulder. "Nonsense, Evie. We all need to help each other on occasion. You have done so much for me and Cassandra since we arrived."

After the maid had gone on her way, Susannah spent her day in the schoolroom. Her charges kept her attention with their escapades, but she did not mind. Their sweetness more than made up for their constant movement.

When she descended for dinner, Susannah was well satisfied. The ride that morning had made each minute of the day better. Before her marriage, she had resided in the country and spent much of her day on horseback. She wondered if Nicholas would object to her repeating the activity each morning.

Nicholas and Jane were waiting for her, and dinner was served at once. When there was a pause in the conversation, Susannah took her courage in her hands and said, "Mr. Danvers, I enjoyed the riding this morning very much. Would it be possible for me to ride again even when the children are not doing so?" She held her breath, her gaze on her employer, anxious for his response.

"The mare you rode this morning is at your disposal, Mrs. Brown," he assured her, appreciative of the pleasure that lit up her face. "Feel free to ride whenever you please. The exercise will be good for the mare."

"Thank you! And Lady Arbor, if I may continue to make use of your habit until mine is delivered, I would very much appreciate it."

"Of course. In fact, this morning so tired me, I may not ride again for several days."

Nicholas looked at his sister in concern. "You do appear rather pale. Are you ill?"

"No. I have just grown lazy," she said with a shrug. "But I have thought what would put me in a better frame."

Nicholas looked at his sister warily. Susannah watched the pair with longing and a little sadness. She had always wanted siblings, someone to confide in and laugh with. Now she was afraid Cassandra was destined to be alone, also.

"A party. I want to hold a party, Nick, so I may see all our friends."

"Could you not pay them a morning call?" her brother asked, his eyebrows raised in protest.

"Do not be a silly, Nick. Of course I will call on them, but it is not the same."

"No, it certainly isn't," he agreed morosely. His wife had insisted on entertaining frequently and had kept the entire household in a constant uproar with her incessant demands. "But if you are not feeling well, how will you be able to handle the details?" he asked, clutching at straws.

"I shall manage. Besides, if I need assistance, perhaps Mrs. Brown will help me." Jane smiled at Susannah.

"Of course I will—"

"No! Mrs. Brown has much to occupy her time. The schoolroom, the household. She has no time for such foolishness!" As the two women stared at him in surprise, Nicholas realized he had betrayed himself. But he could not bear to see Susannah become wrapped up in the very activities that had destroyed his marriage. It was enough that she haunted his every moment without reminding him of the consequences of such beauty.

With two pairs of feminine eyes still on him, he shoved his chair back from the table and stood. "Have your silly party, then. You'll drive me insane with your teasing if you do not." Without another word he strode from the room, leaving stricken silence behind.

"Oh, dear," Jane finally muttered, tears in her eyes. "I only thought to—well, never mind. Even if it causes him pain, I must do this."

"But, my lady—" Susannah began.

"No, you do not understand. My brother's first marriage was horrible, and he has retreated from the world. I cannot permit him to remain unhappy."

Susannah wasn't sure Nicholas was unhappy, but his sister knew him better than she. "If you feel it is for the best for Mr. Danvers, I will be glad to assist you," she said.

"Thank you, dear Mrs. Brown, but I do not want to
upset Nicholas any more than necessary. I am sure to
manage on my own."

Susannah drew a deep breath as she stepped outside the next morning. The sun was just peeking
over the horizon, touching spring's new greenery
with a golden hue. She loved the early morning
air. Its freshness reminded her of her carefree
youth when she had looked forward to the future.
How naïve she had been! Now she must fight for
Cassandra's youth. But for an hour she could return
to that innocence with the wind in her hair, as she
raced across the pasture.

The stableman had her mount ready, as he had the
day before. Standing by him was Nicholas, his gaze
on her.

Susannah came to a halt. She had not seen her
employer since his abrupt departure from dinner
the night before. "Good morning, Mr. Danvers." She
took a hesitant step toward her mare.

"Good morning, Mrs. Brown. I thought you would
not mind some company this morning."

His calm smile reassured her, and Susannah said,
"I would be delighted, sir, if you are not too busy."

"I enjoy a ride early before the troubles of the day
descend."

Since he expressed Susannah's feelings exactly,
the two mounted and rode away from the manor
house in great accord. With only a nod of invitation, Nicholas increased the pace of his animal,
and Susannah followed suit. Soon they were racing
across the pasture, the early spring wind frosting
their faces.

When Nicholas drew rein, he found his governess beside him, her cheeks glowing. "You are an excellent horsewoman, Mrs. Brown. You must've ridden much in the past."

"Oh, yes," she agreed with a laugh. "My aunt used to complain that I spent more time in the stables than I did with my needlework."

"And after your marriage? Did Mr. Brown share your love of riding?"

"We did not have a great deal of time to discover such things, sir." Then, with a rueful look at her companion, she added, "Once I was with child, I was too ill in the mornings and too tired the rest of the day to consider riding."

While Nicholas was occupied with images of Susannah large with child and found himself wishing she were carrying his, Susannah was thinking about what she'd just said. The similarity of Lady Arbor's behavior struck her, and she wondered if the lady might have received her heart's desire.

She darted a quick glance at her companion, wondering if he'd had the same thought, but he was staring down at the reins in his hands.

When he continued to sit his horse, as if he'd forgotten where he was, she said softly, "Sir?"

Jerking his head up, he stared at her before saying, "My apologies, Mrs. Brown. I was lost in thought."

She watched with interest as his cheeks flooded with color.

"While I am apologizing," he continued, "I must do so for my behavior and my words last evening. I do not care for parties, but that does not excuse my response. I have already apologized to my sister, and

I hope you, too, will generously forgive me."

"Of course, sir." Susannah hesitated, but if her surmise was correct, she suspected Lady Arbor would need her assistance. "Do you truly object to my assisting your sister with her preparation? I promise I would not neglect my duties."

To her surprise, his features hardened, and he said sharply, "Of course not, Mrs. Brown. I know how attracted women are to such gaiety. Please plan on attending our little soiree. After all, you must have your reward for your efforts." Without another word or waiting for any reply, he pulled his horse around and raced back the way they had come.

Though her mare begged to join the race, Susannah held her still, staring at the kind, generous, absolutely incomprehensible man riding away from her. She had no intention of attending the party, but he had not given her an opportunity to tell him. Why would he react so to a simple offer to assist Lady Arbor?

Susannah had had little understanding of a man's behavior. Her husband had been a virtual stranger when she married. And having been raised in a totally female household consisting of herself and her aunt, other than servants, she'd grown up without any male influence. It appeared she still knew nothing of those mysterious creatures.

With a shrug, she set her horse at an easy pace, determined to enjoy her ride. She would speak with Nicholas later about the party.

After setting her two students to the task of copying letters under Mrs. Colley's supervision,

Susannah slipped away from the schoolroom and descended to Lady Arbor's bedchamber.

Upon being bade to enter after her quiet knock, Susannah discovered the lady still among the bedclothes, a tea tray beside her. "I'm sorry, my lady, if I am disturbing you."

"No, no, my dear Mrs. Brown. It is only that I am feeling poorly again this morning. I must forgo so much of Cook's excellent dishes from now on. They do not seem to agree with me."

Susannah debated the wisdom of informing Lady Arbor of her speculation but decided against it. After all, it was none of her business. "I came to inform you that Mr. Danvers gave his permission for me to assist you with the party. If you will make up a list of guests, I can write the invitations for you while I am supervising Edward and Theodore."

"How wonderful!" Lady Arbor exclaimed. After setting her teacup on the tray, she swept back the covers and slid from the bed. Pulling her wrapper around her, she slowly walked over to the desk. "I made a list last evening before I fell asleep. I'm sure—" She broke off abruptly and began casting wild looks about the room, holding her mouth with one hand while waving frantically with the other.

Susannah interpreted her gestures rightly and grabbed the washbowl from the dressing table just in time. After Lady Arbor had cast up her accounts with great thoroughness, Susannah helped the trembling lady back to the bed.

"I don't know what is the matter," Lady Arbor protested, embarrassed. "I am never sick." Even as she finished speaking, she burst into tears.

Susannah gathered the sobbing figure into her arms, patting her on the back and murmuring soothing sounds in her ear. When Lady Arbor finally subsided into an occasional hiccuping sob, Susannah said, "My lady, I do not want to raise false hopes, but I behaved just as you have in the early days of my pregnancy."

Lady Arbor raised shocked eyes to Susannah. Even as she watched, those eyes showed wonder and then a rising joy that broadened into a huge smile. "Truly? Even—" she broke off, gesturing across the room to her most embarrassing behavior.

"Many times, I promise," Susannah said ruefully. Hastily she added, "However, it is not proof positive. May I suggest you send for a doctor?"

"Oh, yes! At once! And Peter! I must write to Peter!" Fortunately, before she could rush into precipitious behavior, nature reminded her of her delicate condition. Clutching her stomach, she sank back against the pillows with a groan. "Will this sickness continue until my baby is born?"

"If you are with child, my lady, it will disappear within a few weeks. At least, it did so with me. I'll just ring for your maid to tidy the room, and I will speak to Pritchard about summoning the doctor." Susannah tucked the cover more closely around her and crossed the room to the bellpull.

When Nancy, Lady Arbor's dresser, arrived, Susannah asked her to bring a fresh pot of tea for Her Ladyship after she cleared away the remains of the accident. Then she went downstairs to have a word with Pritchard. After conferring with the butler, Susannah started up the stairs. Her thoughts drifted to the morning she had discovered she was with child, not quite a year ago. The joy Cassie brought her was ever constant. She hoped Lady Arbor was as fortunate.

Before she could reach the top of the staircase to return to Lady Arbor's chamber to ensure she was receiving proper care, Nicholas called to her.

She turned as he came racing up the stairs. "Mr. Danvers? Is aught amiss?"

"That is my question, Mrs. Brown. You summoned the doctor? Who is ill?"

Susannah looked away. "Lady Arbor requested that the doctor call on her."

"Why? What is the matter?"

"I believe you should talk to Lady Arbor, sir."

An exasperated frown marked Nicholas's handsome brow. "Very well, I'll speak to my sister." Without another word, he left Susannah standing at the top of the stairs.

She followed more slowly in his footsteps and waited in the hall, reluctant to intrude on his interview with his sister. A few minutes later he left the room, a broad smile on his face.

"Thank you for your assistance to my sister, Mrs. Brown. She was most complimentary of your help."

"I only hope I am right, sir. I would hate for Lady Arbor to be disappointed."

"You are sure to be correct," he said, a pleased smile on his face. "And there is an added benefit, though you may not see it in such light."

"Pardon, sir?" Susannah asked, frowning.

"An added benefit, indeed. Now there will be no party!"

6

Susannah returned to the schoolroom.

"You have been gone forever, Susannah," Edward complained as she entered.

"Forever, Master Edward?" she asked with a smile, sitting down at the table beside him. Theodore immediately came round the table to lean against her.

"I finished my letters, Susannah. See?"

"Very good, Theodore," she praised, dropping a kiss on his dark hair so like his father's.

"Since we have worked so hard," Edward said, eyeing her speculatively, "*I* think we should have a reward."

Before Susannah could respond, Theodore began jumping up and down. "A story! A story!"

Susannah drew the child onto her lap and put her arm around Edward. "Very well, since you have been so very good." She launched into another story she herself had learned at her aunt's knee.

Mrs. Colley, with Cassandra gurgling in her arms, smiled at the trio. Since Mrs. Brown's arrival, the nursery had become the happiest room in the entire household.

Just as Susannah finished the story, the door opened and Lady Arbor waltzed into the room, beaming at those gathered there.

"It is true! Oh, Mrs. Brown, I am so happy. Colley, did you hear?"

"Hear what, my lady?" the elderly lady asked, a tolerant smile on her face. Lady Arbor was always full of surprises.

"I'm going to have a baby!"

Mrs. Colley hugged her former charge, and for the first time, Lady Arbor noticed the baby in her arms. "Oh, is this your baby, Mrs. Brown? May I hold her? I declare, I know so little about taking care of one. Of course, I will have assistance, but you must instruct me so I will be knowledgeable."

Susannah and Mrs. Colley exchanged smiles as Lady Arbor oohed and ahhed over the baby. Theodore and Edward watched their aunt curiously.

"Aunt Jane is going to get a baby like Cassie?" Edward asked.

"Well, she is going to have a baby, yes," Susannah said cautiously.

"And it can play with Cassie!" Theodore exclaimed.

"Will it be a boy or a girl?" Edward asked.

Susannah hugged the boys close to her. "We will have to wait and see." The thought of where she and Cassie would be when the new baby arrived dominated her thoughts. They were so happy here, but she feared they would not be able to stay much longer. Even if there was no threat to their safety,

Susannah thought, Nicholas might ask her to leave. He did not seem very happy with her lately. She would have to start making inquiries about her future soon.

With the excitement of Lady Arbor's announcement, the boys found it difficult to settle down to work, and Susannah decided it might be a good day to vary their routine and begin their riding instruction.

There were no objections to her plans except from Lady Arbor, who wanted Susannah's attention. She declared she had a million questions to ask her. Susannah promised to come to her as soon as the boys finished their ride.

By dinnertime Susannah was quite tired. She had scarce had time to spend with Cassandra before putting her to bed. Evie had returned to watch over the baby during dinner, though Susannah would have enjoyed a quiet tray in her room.

Instead, she donned her brown wool and made her way to the parlor. There, she discovered Nicholas alone, standing before the fireplace.

"Good evening, sir."

"Good evening, Mrs. Brown," he greeted her, a smile on his face. "We have had an exciting day, have we not?"

"Yes, indeed."

"At least today you have not suffered from the tedium of country life."

Susannah, having sat down on the sofa, hoping to relax for a few minutes, stared at him, confused. "I do not take your meaning, sir."

"I know women find country life tiresome, Mrs. Brown. Particularly a woman with your,

uh, attributes." A chilling smile was on his lips
as his gaze tallied those very attributes, resting on blue eyes, soft, full lips, a slim but
curvacious figure, and, of course, the auburn
curls that lent a vibrancy to her every movement.

Feeling that she'd been insulted but not quite sure
how, Susannah frowned at her employer. "I have
never complained about life in the country, sir. In
fact, I prefer it over London. I have always lived in
the country except for a few months of my life."

He turned his back on her and ambled over to a
window to stare out at his acres. "You are not in a
position at the moment to choose, Mrs. Brown. When
the opportunity arrives, you will be gone." When she
said nothing, he turned to face her. "I only hope you
do not hurt my sons with your departure."

Susannah stood, her shoulders stiff with pride. "If
you are dismissing me, sir, please say so."

His eyebrows rose. "Dismissing you? Why, no,
Mrs. Brown. I have no complaints about your
efforts. But I recognize the impermanence of our
arrangement."

Before Susannah could respond, Jane entered the
parlor, happiness still lighting her features. "Good
evening. I hope I have not kept you waiting. I was
writing Peter, and it was very difficult. I want him
to come at once. Oh, I hope you don't mind entertaining him, also, Nick," she added, as an afterthought,
before continuing, "But I want to tell him face to face,
not in a letter. Perhaps you would read it later, Nick,
to see if I have overly alarmed him."

When she paused to draw breath, she finally recognized the unhappiness on Susannah's face and the

stiffness in her brother's shoulders.

"Is anything amiss?" she asked, looking from one to the other.

"No, of course not, Jane. Mrs. Brown and I were discussing my sons' education." Nicholas approached his sister and hugged her. "Shall we go into dinner?"

This evening he did not extend his other arm to Susannah, as was his custom, but swept his sister ahead of her. That action, as much as his words, was a clear indication that he was unhappy with her presence in his household. Susannah sank her teeth into her bottom lip and fought back the tears. Pride forced her to hold her chin up as she followed them. If he dismissed her, she would find another way to protect her child.

Once they were seated, Jane studied her two companions. "Are you sure there is no problem, Nick? After all, Mrs. Brown is wonderful with Edward and Theodore." A brilliant smile suddenly lit her face. "Why did I not think of it before? When your two have grown too old for a governess, *my* child will be the perfect age. Mrs. Brown, you shall come to me and teach my child!" She smiled triumphantly across the table at Susannah.

Though she felt sure she would not be employed by Nicholas that long, Susannah simply murmured a thank you and concentrated on her soup.

"A nice opportunity, Mrs. Brown, and more to your taste, I'm sure. Lord and Lady Arbor spend a great deal of time in London."

Angry words filled Susannah, and she struggled to contain them. Why did the man persist with the notion that she longed for London? What had she

ever done to convince him of that? Her memories of
London life were not happy ones.

"Now that we are setting up our nursery,
I do not know how often we will return to
London," said Jane. "But our county is very
social, you know. Much more than Nick's." She
took a spoonful of soup before adding, "Oh,
in the excitement I forgot to give you the list
of guests for the party, Mrs. Brown. Perhaps
you might stop by my chamber after dinner.
Then you could begin the invitations in the
morning."

Though she watched the surprise and then protest
in her employer's face out of the corner of her eye,
Susannah said, "Certainly, my lady."

For the first time that evening, Nicholas's attention
was centered wholly on his sister. "What? Surely you
don't intend to go forward with the party now? You
cannot handle all the details in your condition."

"Of course I cannot. But you said Mrs. Brown
might assist me. I'm sure between the two of us
we shall manage." Jane sent a brilliant smile to
Susannah.

Nicholas fumed, trapped by his own words.
"Surely you would not enjoy such a long evening,
Jane."

"But I am having the party for—" She caught
herself before saying too much. "That is, to visit
with my friends. Now I can share with them my
good news. And Peter will have arrived by then,
I'm sure. We shall set it for next Thursday. It will
be perfect!" Since her brother was still frowning at
her, she added, "You will not deny me this treat,
will you, Nick?"

"No, of course not," he agreed before saying with disgust, "I should've known two women would not let a little thing like a pregnancy stand in the way of a party."

Little was said the rest of dinner by either Nicholas or Susannah. Jane, however, chattered on as usual, needing little encouragement in her happiness.

When dinner was ended, Nicholas excused himself, saying he had paperwork to do, leaving the two ladies alone to take tea in the parlor.

"Nick works too hard," Jane complained with a sigh as she sat down. "Please pour, Mrs. Brown. I am feeling particularly lazy this evening."

"My lady," Susannah said, handing the other woman a cup of tea, "are you sure you want to go ahead with the party? Mr. Danvers doesn't seem best pleased with the idea."

"In truth, I do not. I have little interest in our neighbors."

"Then—"

"But I must continue because of Nick. Have you not noticed, Mrs. Brown? In the time you have been here, has my brother had guests? Has he attended any social events? I would wager he has not."

Susannah could not deny her words. It was strange that Nicholas was so totally withdrawn from county society.

"It is all Elinor's fault!" Jane continued hotly. "She was forever entertaining. She even demanded to be taken to London in the midst of the planting season, or during harvest. She cared nothing for Nick's life here."

Suddenly Susannah began to recognize the basis for Nicholas's opinions of women and their dislike

of the country. But *she* had done none of those things
and wasn't sure she liked his assumptions. Nonethe-
less, she felt sorry for him.

"Since her death, Nicholas has had nothing to do
with his neighbors, or anyone else, if it comes to that.
So, you see, I must have the party to bring Nick out of
the doldrums." Jane leaned forward and added in a
low voice, "The real purpose is to find him a wife."

Susannah's smile wavered slightly. She had never
considered Nicholas's remarrying. "Does he—that
is, is he interested in remarriage?"

"No, of course not. That is why this must remain
our little secret. But he is not happy and is alone too
much. A wife is just what he needs. And Theodore
and Edward need a mother."

"They seem very happy to me," Susannah offered,
her feelings slightly bruised.

"Oh, you have made them very happy, Mrs.
Brown, but they need someone permanent in their
lives. A mother, perhaps even more brothers and
sisters. Why, look at how much they enjoy your
baby! Yes, a wife for Nicholas is what is needed."

"Very well, my lady. I will be pleased to assist you
in any way I can."

"Thank you, Mrs. Brown." Jane paused and
looked at the young lady across from her. "May
I call you Susannah? It seems ridiculous to be so
formal after your assistance this day. I feel very
close to you."

"I would be pleased, my lady."

A happy smile on her face, Jane began making
plans for the party. She was totally wrapped up in
them when she suddenly halted, a stricken look on
her face.

"What is the matter, my lady?"

"Oh, Susannah! I had not thought. I am so sorry."

Reaching out to take a hand in hers, Susannah sought the reason for Lady Arbor's distress. "But what is it, my lady? Do you not feel well?"

"No, it is not that. I am asking you to do a great deal of work, but you will not be invited to our party!"

Susannah almost laughed aloud. "Do not concern yourself, my lady. I have no desire to attend the party."

"Are you sure? You are young and quite beautiful. It must grieve you not to be able to dance and flirt and—"

"Truly, my lady, I will be quite content to retire to my chamber when the party begins. Besides, I have nothing suitable to wear to such an event."

That excuse made sense to the fashionably conscious Lady Arbor, much more sense than a young lady having no interest in a party. "That is true. Well, as long as you do not mind."

"I do not. Please don't give it another thought."

After having breakfast alone the next morning, Susannah descended to the kitchen to collect the basket she had ordered prepared for Mrs. Scott, Evie's mother. As she stepped out into the fresh air, the basket on her arm, her employer's voice halted her.

"Mrs. Brown, one moment."

She turned and watched as Nicholas hurried toward her from the direction of the stables. His dark hair ruffled by the early morning breeze, he looked particularly handsome this morning in his leather riding breeches, his broad shoulders encased in a tweed jacket.

"Yes, sir?" She did not look forward to any conversation with him. He appeared to be on the verge of dismissing her.

"You are going to Mrs. Scott's?" he asked as he eyed the basket. After her nod, he continued, "I will escort you, if you do not mind."

Though surprised at his willingness to walk, a necessity as she was not dressed for riding, she accepted his company. In spite of the fact that she seemed to irritate him whenever they spoke lately, she could not dismiss an eagerness to walk with him.

"Of course, sir," she replied sedately.

His intention did not appear to be conversation. With only a nod to her, he took the basket, offered his arm, and set a brisk pace across the green meadow.

Susannah studied him covertly as she hurried to keep pace. Last evening he had appeared angry about the party his sister planned. Perhaps he realized Lady Arbor was matchmaking. No, she thought not. If so, he would have put his foot down and refused to have the party at all.

He glanced her way, and she offered a tentative smile. His response surprised her.

Slowing his pace abruptly, he muttered, "You are a picture of radiant beauty, Mrs. Brown."

She could think of no response other than a mumbled thank you as she felt the skin burn on her cheeks.

"You enjoy walking?"

"Yes—though not as much as riding," she admitted.

"Then why did you not ride this morning?"

"The basket would've been awkward on horse-back." She also did not want to appear to take advantage of her employer's generosity.

"It is kind of you to visit Mrs. Scott," he said, returning to his faster pace.

Rushing again to keep up with him, Susannah only said, "Evie has served me well."

Nothing more was said until they reached Mrs. Scott's cottage. The woman warmly welcomed them, protesting the need for their kindness. Susannah rightly ignored her words and helped her unload the basket Nicholas had placed on the table.

When they finished, the squire insisted the two ladies go outside and sit in the sunshine for half an hour while he remained beside the sick boy.

An hour later, as they took their leave, Susannah noted a more rested look on the mother's face. Nicholas's insistence that she leave her sick child's bedside had been wise. Susannah threw him an admiring look, but he did not see it.

For several minutes nothing was said as they set off on their return walk. When they topped the hill from which the manor house could be seen, sprawled out among its beautifully tended grounds, he drew them to a halt and said, "Mrs. Brown, my sister informed me last evening that she did not think you should attend the party she is giving." He avoided looking at her, his shoulders stiff and his hands rigid.

Susannah watched him, not understanding his intent. "That is correct, sir."

"Well, she was wrong. You shall of course attend the party." He began walking again, perforce pulling her along with him as her hand still rested on his arm.

Stunned, Susannah took several steps before she dug in her heels and pulled her hand from him. When Nicholas turned around to discover the reason for her stopping, she said, "Mr. Danvers!"

"Yes, Mrs. Brown?"

"I have no desire to attend the party."

"So my sister informed me." With a bitter smile on his lips, he added, "Don't be ridiculously proud, my dear. Of course you want to attend the party. If it is a matter of proper dress, have Mrs. Hardy make you a gown, and I will foot the bill."

Susannah was growing tired of bearing the burden for someone else's sins. "I will do no such thing!" she shouted. "Do you think to make my name a byword in the county by paying for my clothing?"

"I have already paid for your riding habit," he reminded her. "You saw nothing wrong with that arrangement."

"Only because you insisted riding was a part of my employment!"

"Your work with my sister is also a part of your employment. It is only right that you attend the party."

"Is Pritchard going to attend the party? What about the parlor maids? I can assure you they will do more work than I for the party. Are they invited?" Her chin was lifted in the air, her eyes sparkling with indignation.

"Do not be absurd!"

"You have not answered my question."

"Of course they will not be invited to the party. They are not of the same level of society."

"I am a governess, Mr. Danvers, not a debutante. I will not attend the party." Susannah would have walked away from the irritating man, but having rightly read her intention, he caught her arm again.

"You have borne your time here in the country well, Mrs. Brown. I am only trying to reward you for your efforts."

"Do me no favors, Mr. Danvers. I am content in the schoolroom." She challenged him with her eyes, daring him to argue with her.

"Are you still hiding from whatever chased you into the country?"

His question surprised her. In fact, in the last several days she had seldom thought of Gerald and the harm he intended. In spite of herself, her face paled.

"Mrs. Brown, if you will tell me of your difficulty, I will help you. In fact, it would be better for all of us if your difficulties were solved before my children grow too attached to you."

"That is the second time you have alluded to my departure, Mr. Danvers. I will leave at once if that is your desire."

Again he held her fast when she would have departed. "I tell you I have no complaints about your work, Mrs. Brown. But I realize you are hiding from someone or something. Perhaps the father of your child? Whether he be Mr. Brown or not?"

Without thinking, Susannah slapped Nicholas's face. "Cassandra is not a bastard!"

Nicholas's hand slid down her arm to grip her wrist in a tight hold, his face still red from her attack.

"I meant no insult. Your beauty is such that few men could resist were they given the opportunity to—to love you." He stared into her eyes, which appeared overly large in her pale face. "I only want to help you, Mrs. Brown."

"I do not need your help, sir," she lied, her teeth worrying her bottom lip. "Nor do I want to attend your party. Let me remain in the schoolroom, sir, please."

His grip on her wrist loosened but did not disappear. A thumb caressed her skin between cuff and glove. "In truth, my dear, you may attend the party with little fear of discovery. Those invited seldom grace London with their presence. No one will know you."

Susannah closed her eyes. Why would he not listen to her? "Sir, I do not want to attend the party."

"All women love parties. Why should you be different?" His words were laced with cynicism.

His insistence pushed Susannah beyond her control. "I am not your wife, Mr. Danvers! I do not live for parties or life in London, and I am tired of being accused of such crimes! I *will not* attend your party!"

She yanked her wrist from his loosened hold, gathered her skirts, and hurried down the hill in the direction of the manor house, leaving a stunned Nicholas to watch her departure.

7

Susannah passed the next day in the schoolroom on tenterhooks every time footsteps were heard in the hall. She feared Nicholas would dismiss her for her outbursts yesterday.

But even as she thought of him, her anger rose again. How dare he assume *she* was like his wife! Besides, it was not a sin to enjoy a party. Some gaiety would not go amiss in Nicholas's life, either. With such thoughts running through her head, she addressed the invitations, eager to demonstrate to a certain person her lack of interest in evening entertainment.

At dinner that evening there was a stiffness in Nicholas's shoulders that warned Susannah she was not forgiven. Almost all of his remarks were addressed to his sister. When she in turn attempted to include Susannah in the conversation, he fell silent.

His behavior irritated Susannah even more. Well, she thought, neither is he forgiven, then. In a spirit of rebellion she turned to Lady Arbor and said, "I finished the invitations today, my lady. Shall I give them to Pritchard for delivery?"

Nicholas glowered at her. Susannah's attempt to share her irritation had been successful.

"Oh, wonderful, Susannah!" cried Jane. "That was very fast work!"

"She probably ignored her duties in the schoolroom," Nicholas muttered.

Susannah bristled at his words, looking directly at him. "I did no such thing. Your children may demonstrate their learning for you, if you wish, sir."

Nicholas remained stubbornly silent, and his sister raced in to fill the emptiness. "Nick meant no such thing, Susannah. Ignore him. And give the invitations to me. I believe I shall deliver several of them in person before sending the rest." She laughed. "I need to catch up on the gossip."

"Feel free to take Mrs. Brown with you when you make your calls," Nicholas said. "I'm sure she can be spared from the schoolroom for such things." With that, Nicholas retired, defeated, a frown on his face for the rest of the evening.

The next several days passed more smoothly. Susannah enjoyed her morning rides alone, though her eager eyes searched the stableyard each morning just in case a companion awaited her. Lady Arbor, after rising late, made several excursions into the neighborhood delivering her invitations, and Nicholas avoided both ladies as much as possible.

After dinner on the third evening, however, as the three of them were sitting in the library, Jane brought up the one topic all three had avoided.

"Nicholas," she said, breaking into his discourse on the planting of the north fields, "I have reconsidered."

"You don't think that is the crop I should plant?" he asked in surprise, knowing her disinterest in anything agricultural.

"No, of course not. I did not even hear—that is, I am talking about our party."

"You've decided not to have it?" he asked eagerly while Susannah stared at her.

"Do not be ridiculous. The invitations have gone out. Of course we must have the party." Jane pursed her lips, a frown on her forehead.

"Then what are you talking about?" her brother asked in exasperation.

"I am trying to tell you, but you keep interrupting." She daintily raised her teacup to her lips while her brother waited for her to continue. "I have visited several of our neighbors delivering the invitations the past two days."

"And they all refused, declaring me an outcast for having refused their invitations?" he asked hopefully.

"You are interrupting me again," she warned him severely.

He raised his hand in surrender and said nothing else.

Susannah watched the pair, ignoring the book she'd been reading, wondering what Lady Arbor had to say. Plans were already in motion for the party. She hoped the changes would not be drastic.

"Very well, I will continue. When I called on our neighbors, they were delighted to discover you were entertaining again. But each lady I chatted with had questions about ... Susannah."

"About me?" Susannah gasped, surprised. "But I am the governess."

Nicholas said nothing, but his features darkened in anger.

"I know, dearest Susannah. But I will confess that I arrived because Mrs. Dilby wrote me about you. And while I have come to accept that there is nothing untoward in the situation, the neighborhood has not."

"The neighborhood can go—"

"Nicholas!" Jane interrupted, sure his comment would not be proper for polite company.

"But I do not understand," Susannah protested. "What has caused the talk? I have done nothing except teach the children."

Jane smiled warmly at her as she tried to explain. "I know, my dear, but, you see, Nick is a widower and you are so lovely. And he has kept you hidden away here."

"That is not true!" Nicholas protested. "I have tried to get the blasted woman to go into Bloomfield. She will tell you!"

"Yes, truly, he has," Susannah said. "But surely no one would suspect—"

"Of course they would," Nicholas interrupted. "The ladies of the county have nothing better to do than to sit around and suspect everyone of anything to their hearts' content." Bitterness filled his voice.

"Now, Nick," Jane said soothingly, "they are not such bad gossips. It is only—well, they are a might jealous, afraid Susannah may have stolen a match on them in capturing the biggest marriage prize between here and London."

"I will not be discussed like some treasure hidden in the garden!" He glared at the two women.

"And I did not become a governess to catch a husband!" Susannah returned, glaring right back.

"Do not become overset. I have a plan." Jane looked at the other two, expecting appreciation.

"A plan?" Susannah asked cautiously, her anger still boiling.

Nicholas was not as subtle. With a groan he protested, "Please, no, Jane. I have been involved in some of your famous plans before. They have all proved to be disasters."

"Nicholas! That is not true," she protested. "Besides, this plan is simple. Nothing can go wrong. Susannah shall attend our party after all."

The other two waited for more details, but Jane remained silent, a beaming smile on her face.

"That is it? That is your plan?" Nicholas demanded.

"Yes. Once the neighbors meet Susannah and realize how good and kind she is, they will not be suspicious of her. And if the two of you show no interest in each other, then there will be nothing for them to see." She paused and eyed her brother warily. "Even better, Nick, if you showed interest in some of the ladies who will be attending—"

"I should've known!" he said disgustedly. "You *are* matchmaking, after I warned you!"

"I am not! But it is the one thing that will convince our neighbors that you and Susannah are not—that you have no interest in her."

Susannah, forgotten for the moment, watched the other two arguing. But she knew their attention would return to her. After all, her appearance at the party was the center of Lady Arbor's idea.

What was she to do? Nicholas had said his neighbors seldom went to London. Could she take the chance that no one had been in London when she made her debut two years ago? Or would remember her even if they were there? Or that they would tell anyone who might get word back to Gerald?

Susannah had accepted that one day soon she and Cassie would have to leave behind the happiness they had found here. But to deliberately expose themselves to the danger lurking somewhere out there seemed foolhardy.

She shivered, remembering the difficult death her maid had suffered in her arms after drinking the poisoned tea. The tea that had been meant for her.

"Mrs. Brown? You are cold?" Nicholas asked, drawing her back to their conversation.

"No, I am fine."

"But you were trembling."

"Never mind, Nick. Susannah, you will do it, won't you?" When Susannah did not immediately answer, Jane added, "Attend our party?"

"I would rather not—"

"And I would rather not have the party at all," Nicholas assured her before she could refuse. "But I must attend, and I believe you also will have to present yourself, Mrs. Brown. After all, my reputation is at stake as well as yours."

"But, sir—"

"I insist," he said quietly but firmly, staring at her.

Susannah dropped her gaze. It seemed she had no choice. If she continued to refuse, it would arouse his curiosity again, and she was even more unsure as to whether she could share her secret with the squire,

as it seemed he had tried to dismiss her several times
recently. Her position might not be as secure as she
once thought.

But what would be the consequences if she attended? She would just have to pray fate would be kind.
After all, they were a long way from London. And
her plans were not secure enough yet to leave.

The next afternoon Susannah led her two students
to the stableyard for their favorite kind of instruction. She was too restless to attend to their sums,
and she needed a break from her troublesome
thoughts. Lady Arbor, having heard the parade of
little feet, guessed their destination and arrived in
the stableyard just as all three had mounted.

"Wait. I will come with you," she called with
a smile. "Will you be patient for your aunt,
Theodore?"

The little boy, astride a fat pony contentedly
munching some oats, nodded. "A'course, Aunt
Jane. See how big I am on my pony?"

"Yes, darling, you appear to have grown amazing-
ly," Lady Arbor assured him with a grin as her mare
was led out of the stables.

"But I am still bigger," Edward bragged. "Shall we
jump a fence today, Sus—Mrs. Brown?" he asked, a
quick glance at his aunt as he almost slipped.

"Not yet, Edward, though you ride excessively
well. I believe Pritchard said they had discovered
some lovely nests in the trees near the west pasture.
I thought we would inspect them today."

Both boys were enthusiastic about her plans, and
the quartet set out on their ride at a sedate pace.
Susannah stayed beside Theodore, her gentle words

of encouragement giving him confidence as he rode. Lady Arbor chatted with Edward, riding ahead of the other two.

When they reached the location of the nests, both boys rode around several trees, searching for any suspicious objects. Jane pulled her mare up beside Susannah.

"My dear, I must talk to you."

"Oh?" she said, but her attention was still focused on the boys. "Over there, Edward. I think in the second tree."

"Yes. Last night when we decided you would attend the party, we did not address a most important issue."

Susannah turned toward Jane and looked at her warily, wondering what bee she had in her bonnet now.

"We did not discuss what your apparel for the party would be. You said you had nothing to wear."

Relief filled Susannah. This issue was easily dealt with. "I shall wear my brown wool, of course, or, if Mrs. Hardy finishes it, my new gown."

"Oh, wonderful. I did not know you had ordered a new gown. I will write Mrs. Hardy a note at once demanding she finish it before the party. Is it silk? What kind of trim are you having?"

Susannah smiled slightly. "My lady, it is a simple gown, a muslin in Bishop's blue, with short sleeves, for spring and summer."

"It does not sound very festive," Jane complained.

"No, but eminently practical for a governess. I needed a gown to spell my brown wool." Unconsciously Susannah sighed. She was coming to hate the brown wool.

"Susannah! I have found one," Edward called.

With a murmured apology, Susannah rode over to the boy's side, and joined by Theodore, they examined the nest Edward had discovered. After the success of their search, Susannah suggested they dismount and enjoy the gingerbread she had brought with them as a treat.

The three turned back to Lady Arbor to find she had been joined by Nicholas. He congratulated each of his sons on his riding skills as they rode up to him.

"Thank you, Papa," Edward said, showing a grin to Susannah.

"Susannah teaches me," Theodore said, wanting to give credit to his teacher. When his father's face grew stern, he looked at his governess anxiously.

"You forgot to call me Mrs. Brown, Theodore," she explained, reaching out to pat his grubby hand. "Your father thinks you are an excellent rider."

"Oh, sorry, Papa. I forgot."

"Please do not forget in the future, Teddy," Nicholas warned, but he smiled kindly at his son.

"We were about to dismount and enjoy Cook's gingerbread, Mr. Danvers. Would you care to join us?"

"Gingerbread just happens to be my favorite. I'm sure Edward will give me his share."

"No, Papa! It's my favorite, too!"

"There is plenty for all," Susannah assured them. She appreciated Nicholas's teasing since it restored the good humor to the group. Before she could dismount, she discovered he had already done so and was waiting to assist her.

"I can manage, sir, but the boys—"

"Will dismount on their own. They must learn to do so. And they most assuredly must learn to assist any ladies riding with them."

"Lady Arbor—"

"Is waiting for you to dismount before I assist her."

With no protest left unanswered, Susannah slid from the saddle into Nicholas's waiting arms, his hands encircling her waist. "Thank you," she said, moving away from him as soon as possible.

She took a bright yellow blanket from the back of her saddle and spread it upon the grass. "We'll rest here in the sunshine. Edward, please ask your father to untie the bag at the back of my saddle."

Soon they were all settled on the blanket, munching gingerbread. Once it had been consumed, however, the children would not willingly stay still and soon were chasing each other around the meadow.

Once the adults were left alone, Jane brought up her earlier concern. "Nicholas, we need your advice. Susannah has nothing appropriate to wear to our party."

Susannah turned a bright red. She hurried to protest. "Lady Arbor, we have no need of Mr. Danvers's opinion. I shall wear my new gown."

Nicholas had been stretched out on his side, his long, powerful body at ease, watching his children cavort nearby. Now he sat up and looked at Susannah. "You have a new gown?"

"I ordered one from Mrs. Hardy, for her to make after she finished my riding habit."

"Then what is the difficulty?" he asked his sister, wanting to drop the subject.

"I fear it is not going to be at all the thing. She said it is quite simple, with no trim. I would feel wretched wearing such a gown when all the other ladies will be dressed to the nines." Indeed, Jane's face reflected such misery.

"But I am not the wife of a peer, my lady. I am simply a governess. And we want to convince everyone of that fact, do we not?"

"Yes, but—"

"I will willingly pay for a new gown, Mrs. Brown," Nicholas offered quietly, interrupting his sister's protest.

"Thank you for your generosity, sir, but I will wear a gown that I have paid for," she said stiffly, avoiding his gaze.

When Jane would've protested again, he said, "Jane, dear, we must allow Mrs. Brown to decide what she will wear. I'm sure she will appear to advantage in her new gown." Before any more could be said, he stood. "Now it is time I returned to work. I cannot laze about in the sun all day like you ladies of leisure." His smile took the sting from his words, and Susannah found herself grinning back at him.

After telling his children goodbye, he rode off across the meadow, Susannah watching him until he was only a speck in the distance.

"Men!" Jane finally said. "What do they know about gowns for a party? Are you sure you do not want a new gown? I will pay for it instead of my brother, if that is the problem."

"Thank you, my lady, for your exceeding generosity, but I shall wear my own gown. I intend to fade into the background as much as possible, and my blue muslin will allow me to do so with no difficulty."

"Yes, that is what I am afraid of," Jane agreed, her only thoughts of fashion and parties.

Susannah, however, felt she had made the correct decision, no matter how much she longed for a beautiful gown. The purpose of her attending the ball was to demonstrate to the county that she was a governess—and nothing else. If she dressed beyond a governess's means, the neighbors would suspect her of illicit goings-on. Besides, Susannah hoped that no guests from London would recognize her in such a plain, but practical, gown.

The thought of illicit goings-on brought a bright blush to her cheeks, but fortunately, Lady Jane was dozing in the sun and did not notice her distraction when Susannah began to daydream about the handsome and confusing Nicholas Danvers.

Nicholas rode away from the impromptu picnic well pleased with Susannah's response. His wife, Elinor, would have never turned down a new gown, whatever the reason. Nor would she have appeared before her neighbors garbed in anything but the latest fashion.

Had he misjudged Susannah? Was it possible she was not like his wife, in spite of her incredible beauty? His mind immediately recalled the warmth of her small waist beneath his hands as he lifted her from her mare. Her breasts had accidently grazed his chest as he'd lowered her to the ground. She'd swiftly moved away, turning her attention to his children.

He rode along, his eyes almost closed as he thought about her. The sun had caressed her auburn hair, turning it to fire. He wondered how it would appear in candlelight, spread about her shoulders. His thoughts dropped from her hair to consider other assets she offered. His contemplations left his mouth watering more than it had for the gingerbread.

Physical discomfort brought on by his imaginings awakened him to his behavior. With a start, he cast such pictures from his mind. He must not think about the woman, he reminded himself. When whatever difficulty she faced was taken care of, she would go away.

He would not be hurt a second time.

8

As the day of the party drew near, Nicholas was surprised at how smoothly his household ran. There seemed to be no rushing about, no disruption of his day, and the servants were not on edge. Everything functioned as normal.

"Pritchard," he said, halting the butler after his delivery of the mail. "Is everything prepared for the party tomorrow night?"

"Yes, sir. Mrs. Brown has everything in hand."

"But I have noticed nothing out of the ordinary. Cook's meals have been all that they should be. The furnishings have not been disturbed. Are you sure she knows what is required?"

"Mrs. Brown is better than a general, Mr. Danvers. She has everything arranged and planned to the last detail. She gave Cook some recipes to prepare in advance, so most of the food preparation is already underway. The cleaning has improved since she spent some time training the maids, so there is not much to be done now. The silver is being polished today, and we will rearrange the furniture tomorrow afternoon." He paused before adding, "It is quite different from when Mrs. Danvers entertained."

His hesitation told Mr. Danvers his butler was fearful of offending his master with his comment about Nicholas's late wife, but the squire could only agree. Susannah appeared able to organize a party without a ripple of disruption in his household. She did not even appear to have neglected her other chores.

Yesterday, he'd passed Evie in the hall, and she'd thanked him for the time off he'd given her to help her mother. While he had no objection to such an arrangement, he had not instigated it. Susannah, of course, had been kind to the young woman, but it meant she'd gone without her assistance during a busy time. Nicholas was beginning to admire Susannah—and not just for her beauty. But he was also cautious.

Elinor had complained for days about the drudgery of preparing for an entertainment, and yet she'd insisted on throwing a party at every opportunity. Susannah, if she was to be believed, had no interest in parties, but she prepared for them quietly and efficiently.

Susannah stood before the mirror in her chamber, staring at her reflected image. Mrs. Hardy was a good seamstress, though, of course, she could not compare to the dressmakers of London. She had carried out Susannah's instructions faithfully, and the result was a simple gown in blue muslin with a high waist and short, puffed sleeves. Certainly it was more flattering than the brown wool.

A sack would be more flattering than the brown wool, she admitted with a wry grin. However, the lack of ornamentation made the gown plain, as Jane had predicted. Dissatisfied, Susannah twitched a sleeve, wondering what she could do to improve her appearance. Or even if she should. She was, after all, proving to all that she was nothing but a governess in this household.

A knock on the door interrupted her thoughts. Lady Arbor entered at once. "Oh, you received your gown from Mrs. Hardy."

"Yes. She sews a fine seam."

"It is just as I said, however. While a serviceable gown, it is not appropriate for evening dress."

"But it must be, my lady. I cannot dress beyond my station. It would destroy all the reasons for my appearance at the entertainment," Susannah said, although her earlier thoughts betrayed her desires.

"I suppose you are right, but it seems a shame. You are such a beautiful woman. You deserve to be dressed in silks and laces."

"I must make do with muslin. At least it is better than my brown wool," she added with a laugh.

Lady Arbor joined in her laughter. There would be no argument there. "I know!" she exclaimed, breaking off her chuckles. "You might improve the appearance of the gown with a lace shawl. It will still be cool in the evenings anyway, so a wrap of some kind will not come amiss."

Susannah considered her reflection in the mirror. Lady Arbor might be right, though, of course, she did not have such a shawl. And she only had one piece of jewelry, a cameo which had belonged to her aunt.

"I had intended to ask you to purchase some ribbon for me to match my gown when you are in Bloomfield today. Perhaps you might also look for a shawl," she suggested hesitantly. One did not easily ask a titled lady to do one's shopping.

"I would gladly do so, Susannah, but I think you should accompany me. Mrs. Hardy has several kinds of shawls, and I am not sure which would serve you best. Surely you can be spared from the schoolroom for an hour or two."

Susannah was torn. In truth, she had been contemplating an outing to the nearby town lately. If she was going to attend the party, what could such an expedition hurt? And yet, the old fears lingered.

"Come, Susannah, say you will go. We will have such fun, at least as much as is possible in Bloomfield." Lady Arbor smiled, clasping Susannah's hand.

"Very well. Let me just check with Evie. She is supervising the boys."

After changing from her new gown back into her brown wool, Susannah ran up the stairs to discover her charges hard at work. She was encouraging Evie to learn to read along with Theodore, and the two were bent over a book of letters. Edward was working on his sums, occasionally lending assistance to the other two in a very superior manner.

When the children learned Susannah was going to town, they asked to accompany her, but she could not let them go without their father's permission. Besides, she did not intend to stay long. After a quick visit to the nursery to see Mrs. Colley and nurse Cassandra before her departure, Susannah descended the stairs to await Lady Arbor.

To her surprise, the other lady was already present. However, she was not alone. Her brother was chatting with her in the hall.

"Ah, Mrs. Brown, I hear you are finally going to make your maiden voyage to the metropolis of Bloomfield," he teased, a warm smile on his face. He was pleased that in this, at least, she was complying with his wishes. And perhaps he had imagined her fear and there was no reason for her and Cassie to be running away.

Susannah could not help but respond to the twinkle in his brown eyes. "Yes, Mr. Danvers. I must make several purchases for the party tomorrow evening. You do not object to my taking time from the schoolroom?"

"Do not be absurd. Have I not offered the same many times? Besides, you have done extra duty in organizing the party. Pritchard tells me you have taken on all the chores with great efficiency."

"Do not be modest, Susannah," Jane chimed in. "You know it is true. I have done almost nothing for the party, and yet preparations are well apace thanks to your help. And I am enjoying myself very much."

"I am glad, my lady." When no one moved, Susannah added, "Is there aught we need to purchase for the household, Mr. Danvers, while we are in town?"

"Pritchard gave me a list of a few things, but I will make those purchases while you and Jane are visiting Mrs. Hardy." He watched as Susannah's eyes widened in surprise. "You did not think I would allow you to visit Bloomfield for the first time without my escort, did you, Mrs. Brown? I intend to treat you and Jane to a sticky bun at the inn when you have finished your shopping."

"But I promised Evie I would return very shortly, sir," Susannah protested. Not only did she want to avoid an overlong stay among strangers, but she also thought it would be best to spend as little time as possible in Nicholas's company. She did not want him to become the target of any danger.

"I believe Evie will spare you long enough for a glass of lemonade, Mrs. Brown." Before she had an opportunity to argue, they heard the carriage approaching. As Pritchard swung open the door, Nicholas gestured to the ladies to precede him.

Nicholas took the seat with its back to the horses, while Jane and Susannah sat across from him. He'd had the top lowered so they might enjoy the sunshine of the spring day.

"I should have brought my parasol, Nick. I did not know you would expose us to the sun. I do not want spots for the party," Jane complained.

"You seldom freckle, sister. Mrs. Brown, however, must suffer from that difficulty since her hair is auburn. Do you wish me to halt the carriage and have the top raised, Mrs. Brown?"

"Oh, no, sir," she replied with a smile. "Unless it truly bothers Lady Arbor, I enjoy the sunshine. It is such a beautiful day."

"Then we shall leave it as it is," he decided, smiling at her enjoyment.

"Well! I think I have been ignored," Jane protested, but she, too, liked the feel of the warm sun.

When they reached the small town of Bloomfield, Nicholas set them down outside Mrs. Hardy's establishment. "I'll return for you in an hour, if that is enough time for you to do your shopping."

"That will be more than sufficient," Susannah assured him after an agreeing nod from Jane.

Inside the shop they found much to occupy them. Not only did Susannah discover a beautiful shawl from Ipswich, its lace intertwined with blue embroidery in the shape of flowers that almost matched her gown, but she also purchased slippers and a ribbon on which she could wear her cameo. Jane found a reticule she could not do without. In a corner of the shop, almost forgotten, it seemed, she also discovered a small doll made from scraps of material. After purchasing it, she handed it to Susannah. "This is for Cassandra."

"Oh, my lady, you should not have," Susannah protested, but already she was stroking the soft form. "She will adore it, I'm sure."

"Baby Cassandra deserves a reward. Colley is using her to teach me about babies, and your child is most patient with my awkwardness."

"Do not worry," Susannah said, patting Jane's hand. "You will be a wonderful mother."

"I hope so. I cannot wait for Peter's arrival so that I may tell him about the baby. I thought he would be here by now."

Susannah smiled at her drooping lips as she took her arm. "I'm sure he will be here soon, my lady."

Jane struggled to smile in return. "Shall we go meet my brother now? I must confess I am looking forward to the refreshments he promised us."

The prospect of lemonade and sticky buns seemed to raise Jane's spirits, and the two ladies bade Mrs. Hardy adieu and stepped out into the sunshine once more.

The brightness of the day in contrast to the dim interior of Mrs. Hardy's shop made it difficult for the ladies to see at first. They paused, waiting for their vision to clear.

"I do not believe my brother has yet returned, Susannah. Why don't we sit upon the bench just here. It is so pleasant today."

Susannah reluctantly followed her companion to the rough-hewn seat near Mrs. Hardy's door.

After several minutes of casual chatter, Susannah felt strangely, as if someone were staring at her. She looked around quickly, but those in sight were paying no mind to the two ladies. A sudden movement to her left drew her attention to the side of the building just in time to see the back of someone as he moved away. Could Gerald have finally found her? Susannah began to fear her worst nightmare might come true. But she must remain calm. After all, she hadn't actually seen anyone following her, and no one had approached them.

"Is something wrong, Susannah?" Jane asked. "You are trembling."

"No. Does—does Bloomfield have many strangers visit?" Susannah tried to sound casual, but she felt unnerved and suspiciously watched the other patrons.

"Bloomfield? Gracious, no. Why would anyone come to Bloomfield?"

Before Susannah could respond to Jane's remarks, Nicholas came strolling pleasantly down the street, although he looked thoughtful and a little tense. "My apologies, ladies. Several people wanted to lodge complaints with me, so I was delayed." He reached out to take their packages. "Shall we go to the inn? I have requested the parlor be set aside for our use."

Jane sprang to her feet. "I vow, shopping always makes me hungry. I am ready for my treat."

Susannah rose more slowly, her eyes again scanning the street.

"Mrs. Brown?" Nicholas said. When she finally looked at him, he said, "Are you ready to go to the inn?"

"Yes, of course. I—I was just looking at Bloomfield. After all, it is my first visit."

"Two minutes should be sufficient," Jane said drolly and led the way across the dusty street to the Duck's Tail Inn.

Once inside, Susannah relaxed somewhat. The threesome settled down at the table and took refreshing sips of the lemonade Nicholas had promised.

"What problem did someone have to report? Anything serious?" Jane asked.

"There has been a stranger here about, asking questions," Nicholas replied. He studied Susannah, awaiting her reaction, but was still taken aback by the momentary look of stark terror that came into her eyes.

In her agitation she knocked over the glass of lemonade. Jane shrieked and jumped aside to avoid the rush of liquid. Susannah, too, leapt to her feet, searching for something to stem the flow.

Nicholas shouted for the maid. When she scurried into the room, she took immediate stock of the problem and set about putting everything to rights. In no time all were seated once again, and Susannah had a fresh glass of lemonade.

"What were you saying about a stranger, Nick?" Jane asked. "It is bizarre, but I just told Susannah that we never have strangers here in Bloomfield."

"Why would you say such a thing?" he asked, still closely watching Susannah.

"Because Susannah asked if we ever had any strangers."

"You have an interest in strangers, Mrs. Brown?" he asked.

Susannah took a sip of her fresh glass of lemonade, careful to avoid Nicholas's gaze, though she could feel his dark eyes burning into her. "No, sir. It was an idle question."

He did not believe her words, but he had nothing with which to accuse her. In truth, the concerns several citizens had presented him made him uneasy, and Susannah's reaction confirmed that there was indeed a problem. While strangers were rare, they were not unheard of in Bloomfield. But this particular stranger seemed intent on asking questions. Yet he vowed he knew no one in the area and was simply traveling around England. Who was Susannah hiding from?

Nicholas studied the delicate face of the woman across from him. He had wanted her to come to Bloomfield, to face the problem, or person, she was avoiding, but he did not want her hurt. And the look of terror on her face made him fear for her safety.

Only when the carriage turned onto the neatly groomed drive did Susannah relax. As she rode toward the manor house, her head hummed with questions. Had the stranger been looking for her? Would Gerald come himself?

An even more difficult question presented itself. Must she take Cassandra and leave? Her heart ached at the thought. They were so happy here. She did not want to leave. Her gaze focused on Nicholas as he chatted with his sister.

Perhaps she could remain a little longer, she pleaded with her conscience. Surely another week of comfort would not hurt. It would take longer for the man to report back to Gerald and for him to choose a way to dispose of her.

There was no doubt in her mind that her death was the ultimate goal. Hers and eventually Cassie's. Gerald, her brother-in-law, had inherited the title and the entailed estates from Reginald, but *her* fortune and lands had not been entailed and had returned to her control. Without her money, the home of the Earls of Craven was worthless. Her husband had married her for her wealth. He said he would use her money to turn his estate into a prosperous one once more.

However, after his death, she discovered he had spent funds on his own entertainment and enrichment and had done little to improve his estate. She also discovered that his brother intended to have everything, including her wealth.

The first attempt on her life had been late at night, before the birth of her child, only a month after her husband's death. Unable to sleep, she frequently walked down to the library for new reading material. At the top of the stairs a strong hand had pushed her. Only because she'd been holding on to the banister had she been saved from a disastrous fall. As it was, the event had brought on Cassie's birth.

Even as she went through the throes of childbirth, Susannah had tried to determine who would want her injured or even dead. Her sister-in-law, Gerald's wife, hovered over her, but the doctor remained with her, also. Though she could not yet bear to believe her husband's family might wish harm to her and her child, she was uncomfortable around the new Lady Craven.

She kept to her rooms the first week after Cassie's birth, trying to persuade herself that nothing was wrong. However, toward the end of the week, her maid brought up a tea tray for her. Since her appetite had disappeared, she refused the tea or the cakes that accompanied it. Rather than have it go to waste, however, she told her maid to enjoy the offerings. Within minutes the woman died a painful death in Susannah's arms, poisoned by the tea.

Knowing for certain then that someone wished her harm, Susannah had started down the stairs to seek out assistance when she heard her brother-in-law and his wife in the master suite, discussing how they would spend her money. She fled to her room in a state of panic, realizing she had no one to turn to. She was completely alone, and that left her no choice but to take control of her own life. And Cassie's. But who would believe that the present earl was trying to kill her? It seemed her only hope was to escape.

"It appears we will have a guest for dinner," Nicholas said, waking Susannah from her musings. She jerked her head around, fearing the stranger had appeared on Nicholas's doorstep.

Instead, a stylish carriage was just pulling away from the front door, and Jane screamed with joy.

"Peter! Peter is here!" She grabbed the carriage door as if she would leap down before the carriage had halted, but her brother prevented her from doing so.

"Come now, Jane. You have waited so long, another minute will not harm you."

Lord Arbor, having heard the new arrivals, stepped back outside and waved to them. When Nicholas's carriage halted, the gentleman was at its door to assist his wife down.

"Jane! Is aught the matter? I could not make head nor tail of your letter! Are you well?" All the questions were asked with his wife gathered into his arms, his cheek pressed against hers.

"Oh, Peter! I am so glad you are here!"

"As I am, love," he assured her huskily, "but you have not answered my questions."

Nicholas descended from the carriage and then assisted Susannah down. Turning to his brother-in-law, he said, "I think Jane would like to explain everything to you in private, Peter. Why don't you go to her chamber. I'll have tea sent up."

Lord Arbor searched his brother-in-law's face and then relaxed when he saw the smile. With an arm still holding his wife close, he nodded his thanks and led Jane into the house.

Susannah stood watching them go, her heart heavy. Her marriage had never had such warmth or caring. How wonderful it must be to have a husband who loved and adored his wife. Unconsciously her eyes sought out Nicholas. He offered his arm to escort her into the house, a light in his eyes that brought a blush to her cheeks. But the moment passed quickly when Susannah remembered the potential danger she might bring to the people she'd come to love like a family. Susannah knew the time had come for her to make plans for her and Cassie's departure—as soon as the party was over.

9

Susannah studied her reflection in the cheval glass. The Bishop's blue gown matched her eyes perfectly and complemented her auburn curls. Wrapping her new lace shawl about her shoulders, she touched the cameo threaded on a blue ribbon about her neck. As always when she wore the cameo, she thought of the woman who had loved and raised her and arranged her marriage. Aunt Molly had hoped Susannah's husband would care for her charge as she had done.

Sighing, she turned away from her image. At least her aunt had not lived to know what a dismal failure her marriage had been. After seeing the love Lady Arbor and her husband shared, amply demonstrated at his arrival and again at the dinner table last evening, Susannah regretted her own marriage, except for Cassie.

Susannah looked down and traced the carved face with her fingers. Its delicate beauty was her only treasure. All the other jewels had been left in her man of business's safe in London, but the cameo was too precious to leave behind. In any case, it was modest enough for a governess.

And that was the role she must remember to play this evening. A governess. Nothing more. Resolutely she turned and left her room. She had put off her descent until after most guests had arrived. She did not want anyone to think she was attempting to fill the role of hostess.

The noise of many voices filled her ears as she slowly came down the stairs. She hoped to slip into the room unnoticed and occupy a hidden corner for an hour before returning to her chamber. Since she knew no one other than her host and hostess and Lord Arbor, she felt sure her plan would work.

The rooms gleamed with candlelight and furniture polish, and the elegantly dressed guests mingled as the musicians tuned their instruments. Susannah did not see her host and breathed a sigh of relief. She had avoided him, other than at meals, since their outing to Bloomfield. With the minimum of notice, she joined the guests.

However, she had not counted on Lady Arbor's exceptional good humor. No sooner had Susannah entered the room than Lady Arbor signaled for Susannah to join her. Happiness flowed from Jane in all directions now that her husband was with her.

"Susannah, you must meet our neighbors." She scarcely drew breath, giving Susannah time only to reluctantly nod before she said, "Mrs. Brown is the most wonderful governess. Edward and Theodore just adore her. I have already enlisted her services for *our* child. By then Nicholas's two will be ready for a tutor."

When someone evidenced surprise that Lady Arbor was *enceinte*, she launched into her announcement again, giving excessive credit to Susannah for caring for her.

The only name Susannah recognized when introductions were made in the group of ladies was Mrs. Dilby, the lady whose letter had brought Lady Arbor flying to her brother's rescue.

"It is a pleasure to meet you, Mrs. Brown," the woman purred, but Susannah noted the avid interest in the woman's gaze. "Are you a widow?"

"Yes, I am."

"But I understand you have a child?"

"Oh, yes, she has the most darling baby," Jane enthused. "I have been playing with her so I will know how to care for my own baby."

"How nice," Mrs. Dilby said dismissively. Looking at Susannah, she asked, "It must have been difficult to obtain a position with a baby."

"Yes." She wanted to add that it had been most kind of the squire to employ her, but thought better of it, afraid she'd be misunderstood.

"Of course, with your, uh, assets, I suppose it is easier for you than some." The lady's eyes did a deliberate inventory of Susannah's body.

"Oh, Susannah is wonderfully talented in caring for children. And can you believe it? Little Theodore is already learning French! I vow I never learned a word of it, and my three-year-old nephew is just chatting away." Jane's happiness did not allow her to realize the true meaning of the woman's words, but Susannah pressed her lips together and tried to control her rising anger.

Fortunately, Jane's attention was caught by her brother from across the room. "Oh, Susannah, Nicholas is signaling for the music to begin. Would you inform the musicians, please?"

Gladly, Susannah left the circle of women, happy to escape before Mrs. Dilby pushed her to a retort that would be unwise. Perhaps the lady would be distracted by the music. The doors between the morning room and the parlor had been opened and part of the furniture cleared away to allow for some dancing. At one end several tables had been set up for cards for some of the older members who preferred that socialization instead of dancing.

Susannah spoke to the musicians and then moved on to the dining room to check the buffet as the music started, as she had no intention of taking the floor herself.

Pritchard, of course, had everything well in hand, leaving Susannah nothing with which to occupy her time away from the party. She stepped back into the parlor. It was only by chance, of course, that her gaze fell immediately on Nicholas swinging a beautiful woman around the small dance floor. Her petite blond figure contrasted charmingly to Nicholas's manly form and raven locks.

For all Nicholas's disparagement of town life, Susannah thought he was dressed as modishly as any man-about-town. He must go to London occasionally if only to replenish his wardrobe.

She noted his social skills were quite adequate, also, as the blonde smiled longingly up at him. Turning away, Susannah stifled the irritation she was feeling. After all, Lady Arbor had never said her brother *could* not enjoy society, only that he *would* not.

When Susannah would have slipped into a chair near a potted plant, she found her way blocked by Mrs. Dilby.

"My dear Mrs. Brown. I promised Lady Arbor I would introduce you to some suitable partners. After all, we would not want to waste such beauty on a wallflower, now, would we?"

"Thank you, Mrs. Dilby, but I do not care to dance."

"Nonsense. I saw you watching our host with great envy. I assumed you were eager to take the floor yourself." She paused to arch up an eyebrow. "Unless I mistook your look for one of envy of his partner?"

Anger flared through Susannah, but she coolly stared at the lady. "No, Mrs. Dilby, that is not the case. It is just that as governess, I did not feel it proper for me to dance."

With a humorless smile the lady replied, "In London that would be true, but we are not so formal here in the country. Come. I have just the partner for you."

Though Susannah would've preferred a rapid return to her chamber, she had little choice but to follow Mrs. Dilby. When the lady stopped in front of a stooped gentleman with an ear horn, Susannah knew she had an enemy for life.

"Mr. Greyson!" Mrs. Dilby shouted. "I've brought you a partner for the next dance!"

"Hey?" he bellowed, even as his gaze lit on Susannah with appreciation.

"Dance!" Mrs. Dilby shouted even louder. "She wants to dance with you!" Unfortunately, the musicians played the last note of their song just as she began her second sentence, and every word was heard throughout the downstairs.

Once Mr. Greyson understood Mrs. Dilby's words, there was no stopping him. He sprang to Susannah's side with more energy than she would have thought possible and immediately pulled her close to him. Before Susannah could even guess his intent, he dragged her to the dance floor and began moving in circles, holding her much too close, as if the music were continuing.

"I love to waltz!" Mr. Greyson shouted, a broad smile on his face.

Though she was thoroughly embarrassed, Susannah could not have disappointed the elderly man. His pleasure was enjoyable even if his dancing was not, and she did not want to be rude to the squire's guest. With her chin uplifted, she smiled back at him and pretended the floor was not bare of dancers and the pair of them were not the cynosure of all eyes.

Nicholas had followed Susannah's movements from the moment she entered the party. He had wanted to introduce her to his friends, to smooth the way for her, but the foolish gossip had tied his hands. He remained at a distance and hoped Jane would not forget her.

When Mrs. Dilby approached Susannah while he was occupied with Miss Winston on the dance floor, he'd hoped for once the woman would have a charitable bone in her body and be kind to his governess.

He should have known better.

Now, when he realized what was about, he swiftly moved to the musicians and commanded a waltz. Nicholas signaled to his brother-in-law even as he requested the nearest lady's hand for the dance, and soon there were three couples on the floor, swaying to the music.

The laughter that had begun was quickly stifled, and other couples joined in until the awkward moment had passed away. However, Nicholas still watched Susannah from the corner of his eye and admired the dignity and grace with which she handled the situation.

Susannah breathed easier, grateful for her employer's quick thinking. It would have been difficult to sustain her pride for the entire dance. Though how Mr. Greyson would know when the music ended, Susannah did not know. That thought had her holding back a grin that threatened to break into hysterical laughter just as she swung around face to face with Nicholas.

Without thinking, she mouthed the words *thank you* to him, before Mr. Greyson swung her away. When the music ended, the couple nearest them stopped and applauded the music. When Mr. Greyson continued to move, the gentleman tapped him on the shoulder and indicated he should applaud. Susannah smiled her gratitude to the man.

"Thank you, sir," she said to Mr. Greyson and started to move away.

"Mrs. Brown?" The gentleman who had stopped their dance was bowing to her. "I am Mr. Robinson, Danvers's nearest neighbor. May I present my wife?"

"How do you do? I am pleased to meet you," Mrs. Robinson, a pretty brunette, said. "We have heard wonderful stories about how happy you have made Theodore and Edward."

"Thank you, Mrs. Robinson. They are delightful boys."

"Perhaps after Lady Arbor's departure, Nicholas could spare you to take tea with me one afternoon."

The invitation eased the knot of tension that had risen in Susannah, and she smiled warmly. "Thank you, Mrs. Robinson. I would be delighted."

"James, darling, why don't you fetch us both some punch. I'm sure Mrs. Brown would like a rest after that strenuous dance." The lady tapped her husband on the arm, sending him toward the dining room and drawing Susannah down beside her in the chairs against the wall.

The next few minutes were enjoyable as Lucy Robinson made small talk with Susannah and introduced her to several of the other neighbors, making Susannah feel comfortable and welcome. When the music began again, there were several gentlemen eager to request her hand. When she hesitated, Lucy insisted she dance again, and Susannah capitulated.

In truth, she enjoyed dancing, and not to dance would be to allow Mrs. Dilby to think she had embarrassed her. Susannah accepted the first gentleman's hand and moved gracefully to the floor.

Nicholas watched the circle of friends even as he discussed agriculture with an older gentleman. Envy rose in him as Susannah took the floor with Samuel Lemmett, a young man he'd watched grow up. Susannah could not possibly enjoy dancing with Samuel. He was still wet behind the ears. When Nicholas realized the path his thoughts were taking, he forced his attention to wheat, and not the swaying figure in Bishop's blue.

Mrs. Dilby watched the young governess. She detested being laughed at, and her attempts to humiliate Susannah had failed miserably. Instead, she had been praised by several people for her tolerance of Mr. Greyson. There had even been cold stares sent Mrs. Dilby's way.

Well, she would not be routed by a young woman who thought herself better than she should be. After all, she was just a governess!

If she could not ruin the beauty's reputation one way, she could always try another. With purpose in her steps she moved to the nearest group of women to plant her barbed seeds of gossip.

From Mr. Lemmett's hands Susannah next took the floor with Mr. Jacobs, an older, sophisticated gentleman. His dance skills were considerably above Mr. Lemmett's, and Susannah relaxed in enjoyment.

"You are an exquisite dancer, Mrs. Brown."

"Thank you, Mr. Jacobs. You are quite accomplished, also."

"Years of practice in London, my dear. An unattached man is forever being pressed to partner someone."

Susannah paled as she considered his words. She had hoped the guests would not be familiar with London society.

"Have you attended a Season in London, Mrs. Brown? I feel as if I've met you before, though I cannot imagine ever forgetting someone of your beauty."

Susannah avoided his eyes and instead concentrated on her partner's cravat. "No, sir. Do you have plans to go to London this year?"

"Oh, yes," he assured her with a bored air. "I go every Season. My sister is launching her youngest this year, so I must lend my support."

"I'm sure you will be of great assistance, sir," Susannah said, praying the music would end soon. When it did, she moved swiftly to the edge of the dance floor, but her partner followed her.

"Where is your home, Mrs. Brown? Perhaps I encountered you on some of my travels, because I distinctly recall your charming face. Only I cannot remember where."

"My looks are common enough, sir," she asserted. "I am sure you are confusing me with another. If you will excuse me, I must see if Lady Arbor is growing tired," she hurriedly added before the man could ask any more awkward questions.

Lady Arbor was seated across the room, chatting with her husband and brother, and Susannah headed in their direction. However, she was not so absorbed that she failed to notice the stares and whispers among several ladies as she passed by. Surely Mr. Jacobs could not have already speculated about her identity? She had just parted from him. Could someone else have recognized her?

She decided she should ask Lady Arbor for permission to retire. And reluctantly she admitted she must begin to secure the details for her departure before Mr. Jacobs or someone else recognized her and reported to her brother-in-law.

"Lady Arbor, I—" she began as she reached the trio.

"Mrs. Brown, are you all right?" Nicholas interrupted. "You appear pale."

"Yes, Susannah, sit here with me," Jane suggested, patting the seat beside her.

"My lady, if you do not mind, I would prefer to retire. Unless I may assist you in some way."

"The party will continue for some time," Nicholas said. He was not happy to be ignored. "Surely you would like to dance again?"

"No, sir, I would prefer to withdraw to my—"

"Mrs. Brown, you are such a divine dancer," Mrs. Dilby squealed as she approached the quartet. "I have enjoyed watching you so much. However, I'm sure you would show to greater advantage with a better partner."

Susannah was not fooled by the woman's complimentary words. With a quiet thank you, she turned her attention back to Lady Arbor.

Mrs. Dilby, however, would not be ignored. "Mr. Danvers, you could show Mrs. Brown's skills to advantage. Why do you not partner her this next dance? Then everyone will realize what an exquisite dancer she is."

"Thank you for your compliments," Susannah rushed to say before the squire could respond, "but I do not care to dance anymore. I find myself fatigued from my earlier efforts." She did not want to feel Nicholas's arms around her in a room full of strangers.

"I begin to wonder at your avoidance of each other," the woman persisted with a coy look directed toward her host. "Perhaps the two of you have something to hide."

Nicholas's handsome features grew austere as he stared at his guest. "Mrs. Dilby, I intend to dance with Mrs. Brown, not because of your distasteful assumptions, but because I do not want to deny myself that pleasure." With a brief bow he extended his arm to Susannah. She placed her hand on his sleeve, obeying the command in his eyes.

"Rest assured, Mrs. Dilby," he added before leading Susannah to the dance floor, "I will not forget your behavior this evening." The chill of his words brought fear to the older woman's face. She finally seemed to realize she had overstepped the mark.

Ignoring Mrs. Dilby's cry of protest, Nicholas signaled the musicians to begin a waltz, and his arms encircled Susannah. At his touch she trembled and closed her eyes. When she opened them, she discovered him smiling down at her.

"You must appear to enjoy our dance, Mrs. Brown, but not too much," he said softly. "I'm afraid Mrs. Dilby has done her best to blacken our names."

"Yes, Mr. Danvers," Susannah agreed, making a conscious effort to smile calmly in spite of the turmoil his touch created.

After several minutes of dancing, he said, "Mrs. Dilby is correct about one thing. You dance divinely."

"Thank you."

"You must have attended many parties to be so well trained."

In spite of her resolve to remain calm, Susannah heard the distaste in his question. "No more than any young lady going through the Season," she snapped.

There was a perceptible pause in his movement that disrupted their steps before he recovered. Susannah's cheeks flushed as she realized what she'd said.

"I did not know you had enjoyed a Season. It must have been two or three years ago when my wife was increasing and then ill, because I attended at least part of every Season prior to then." Nicholas tried to imagine how different his life might've been had he remained a bachelor until he met the beauty in his arms. Her soft words drew him from his fantasy.

"Please, Mr. Danvers, you must not—do not mention my past to anyone." The plea in her sky-blue eyes would have moved a stone to compassion.

"I will not do so, of course, Mrs. Brown, but running away is not an answer. If you will tell me why you are hiding so far from London, I will do my best to assist you."

She stared over his shoulder and resolutely shook her head. She could think of nothing he could do to stop Gerald, and even the thought of shifting her burden to Nicholas's capable shoulders weakened her courage.

"There must be a solution to whatever you fear," he added insistently.

"I know of no solution to murder, sir," she whispered fiercely.

10

Nicholas's hand tightened spasmodically on her back, pulling her closer to him. "You have committed murder?" he whispered hoarsely, his eyes widened in shock.

"No!" Susannah gasped. "*I* have done nothing wrong." The music ended and she stepped out of his arms. "Please, sir, may I retire?"

Though he wanted to pull her from the room to his library, where they could be private, Nicholas knew they would both have to hide their desire to depart. "I'm sorry, Susannah," he said in a low voice, unaware he had used her first name. "We must both remain here. For either of us to leave now would occasion talk. But we will discuss this later. I will not let the subject rest." When Susannah did not object, he took her arm and escorted her back to his sister.

"Nicholas, what is going on? You were not supposed to show your interest in Susannah! Everyone has been staring and whispering!" Though she was also whispering, Lady Arbor's agitation was easily observable.

Nicholas drew a deep breath before saying quietly, "We enjoyed our dance very much, thank you, Jane. Are you willing to take a chance on my dancing skills?"

"But, Nicholas—" Jane began.

"Of course she is," her husband intervened. "And I shall solicit Mrs. Brown's hand, if you are willing," Lord Arbor said with a smile. "It is a country dance, one of my favorites."

"I would be delighted, my lord," Susannah replied, relief evident in her face. Whether she was pleased to escape his presence or his sister's questions, Nicholas did not know.

"We will talk later," Lady Arbor assured her brother as she stood to take his hand.

"There will be a number of private conferences," Nicholas murmured under his breath.

The dance movements separated the two of them but brought Nicholas face to face with Susannah once more. He could almost feel an intentness in the watching guests. Offering her a calm smile, he only hoped she would respond in kind. Even as she did so, Nicholas considered again her shocking words at the end of their dance.

Hiding his impatience, he turned from Susannah to Lucy Robinson and then on to the next lady in line, but his thoughts remained with Susannah. He had imagined many reasons for Susannah to hide in the country, but murder had never crossed his mind.

What could she have meant? Had she seen a murder? Or even worse, had someone threatened her? He could not imagine anyone wanting to extinguish such a beauty, as one would a candle. The idea of Susannah lying lifeless filled him with such unexpected anguish, he stopped in mid-dance, drawing immediate attention to himself.

"Mr. Danvers?" elderly Mrs. Bonney asked. "Is anything amiss?"

He stared down at the little lady, surprised. "Why, no, Mrs. Bonney. I was just—just distracted for a moment." He offered his arm to his neighbor and swung her in the appropriate circle, but a fierce frown remained on his brow.

Susannah, too, had difficulty concentrating on the dance steps. What a disaster the evening had turned out to be. First Mrs. Dilby tried to work her mischief; then Mr. Jacobs thought he recognized Susannah. While he had not yet connected her to the naïve young lady she'd been several years ago, it was probably only a matter of time.

What happened with Nicholas Danvers was her own fault. She'd wanted to prove to him she was not like his wife. Instead, all she'd accomplished was to reveal too much about her own past. She refused even to consider why it was important that he think her different from Elinor Danvers.

She was unaware of sighing until Lord Arbor said quietly, "No sighs, my dear. Put a smile on your face so people will believe you are content with me as your partner."

Looking up at the kind man, Susannah murmured, "Of course I am pleased with you as my partner, my lord." The smile that followed was not her best, but it passed muster for the curious stares she encountered as she moved around the room.

* * *

When Nicholas turned from saying good night to his last departing guest, he discovered his sister had retired an hour earlier, exhausted by the evening and her condition. Mrs. Brown must have slipped away at the last minute, because only Lord Arbor remained downstairs.

"A delightful evening, Nick," Lord Arbor commented.

Nicholas frowned at his favorite brother-in-law. "That is not exactly how I would describe it."

Lord Arbor studied him before saying, "If I can be of any assistance, Nick, you know you have only to say the word." Lord Arbor was several years younger than the squire and a peer of the realm, but the two had become fast friends during Peter's courtship of Jane.

"Thank you, Peter, but I am not sure what the difficulty is, much less what to do about it." He turned toward the library. "Would you care for a drink before you retire?"

Lord Arbor nodded his agreement, and the two entered the library. As he sat down, he said in an offhand manner, "Mrs. Brown is a charming lady."

Nicholas arched one eyebrow in amusement. "Quite."

Grinning, Peter said, "All right, I will admit that I am curious. I seem to remember having met her, but I cannot think where."

"She admitted tonight that she had a Season." Nicholas watched Peter's face intently for a reaction.

Peter frowned, concentrating. Suddenly his eyes widened. "Of course! She was an heiress."

"What are you talking about? She is working as a governess."

Rising, Peter paced across the room as he thought. "I am positive she is the same girl, but I cannot remember her name. She was married very soon after she was presented. Her birth is good but not noble, and she married a peer." He turned an exasperated face to Nicholas. "I can't remember his name or title, either. He ran in a different crowd. But everyone joked about how fortunate he was to get such a beauty *and* a fortune, too."

"What happened to him?" Nicholas's hand clenched his glass tightly as he waited for a reply.

Peter sat back down with a sigh. "I don't know that, either. I seem to remember catching a glimpse of him late last Season, but his wife was not with him. What did Mrs. Brown tell you?"

"That she was married to a soldier who was killed on the Continent."

Peter shook his head. "No, that can't be right. She must've—"

"Lied. Women do that rather frequently," Nicholas remarked bitterly.

"Come now, Nick, that particular talent is not limited to the female only."

"No," Nicholas admitted as he stood and strode over to stare out into the darkness. "But females are particularly good at it."

"Some. But Mrs. Brown is not like your wife, Nick. I have only known her a little more than a day, but she seems valiant, caring, and intelligent. Certainly your children believe her to be perfect."

"And I should base my judgment on the beliefs of children?" Nicholas asked sarcastically, turning around to stare at Peter.

With a sympathetic smile he replied, "No, my friend, you should base your judgment on what your heart tells you."

Nicholas almost spilled his drink before he could hide his response. "My heart has nothing to do with what we are talking about!" Before Peter could answer, he hurriedly added, "We are discussing Mrs. Brown's suitability as a governess . . . and her reasons for hiding in the country."

"Have you asked her for reasons?"

Nicholas nodded. "But until tonight, she only said she was widowed and needed to support herself and her baby."

"Until tonight?"

"I promised her I would say nothing. I should not have even told you that she had a Season." He stared moodily into his glass. "But I intend to question her in the morning." The firm resolve in his voice made Peter smile. He had seen prior demonstrations of Nick's determination.

"If I may be of assistance, just let me know," he said as he stood. Setting his glass down on the table beside his chair, he added, "Jane and I would like you to be happy, Nick."

"I am fine as I am, Peter, as I have told Jane innumerable times. It is Mrs. Brown who needs our concern at this moment."

Peter nodded and smiled, but as he left the room, he muttered under his breath, "Particularly yours, my friend."

*   *   *

In spite of her late night, Susannah rose early. She needed exercise to clear her mind, and she had a lot of planning to do.

Sacrificing the joys of a morning ride in order to avoid her employer, Susannah turned to the squire's extensive gardens for a walk. Dismay filled her as she chanced upon a charming alcove surrounded by hedges and rose bushes only to discover Nicholas and Lord Arbor seated on a stone bench deep in conversation. She instinctively pulled back, but it was too late. The men had already seen her.

"Good morning, Mrs. Brown," Lord Arbor called cheerfully. "We did not think either of you ladies would be up and about after your late night."

"I only desired a bit of fresh air. Do not let me disturb you." With a nod she continued to walk.

Nicholas, having stood with his brother-in-law, stared at her, frustration on his face. "We will walk with you," he said firmly, allowing no argument, and sending her a knowing look.

Susannah only nodded, since she felt she had no choice. At least Lord Arbor would accompany them, which would prevent her employer from asking any awkward questions.

Nicholas was thinking the same thing, but he was not pleased with the results. He had scarcely slept, worrying about her words the evening before. The urge to protect her was overpowering all rational thought. Last evening, whether he wanted to admit it or not, he realized just how much he cared for Susannah when he pictured her lifeless.

Not that his feelings would affect his behavior. After all, it was his duty as a gentleman and her employer to protect her. When he did so, then whatever she was hiding from would go away and so would Susannah. And the sooner the better, he assured his aching heart.

Susannah looked at neither gentleman as they moved among the newly budding plants. Any hope of making firm plans for her departure must await the privacy of her chamber.

"You are an excellent dancer, Susannah—I mean, Mrs. Brown," Lord Arbor said pleasantly. "Forgive me. Jane always speaks of you as Susannah."

"I do not object, my lord."

"Then I, too, will call you Susannah," Nicholas said abruptly. "After all, I have known you longer than Peter."

Susannah avoided looking at him. "Certainly, sir."

Somehow, her response did not please him, even though she had agreed to his request. Nicholas stared at her, his look tracing her delicate profile.

"Jane also says she has asked you to come to us when Nick's boys are too old for your care."

"Yes, my lord, she did." Susannah said nothing more. After all, her plans did not include being here next month, much less in several years.

"That will not be for some time," Nicholas inserted, irritation in his voice. "After all, Teddy is only three. He will need a governess until he is eight, at least."

Susannah said nothing, continuing to stroll down the gravel path. The fresh air was invigorating, but its benefits were lessened by the tension in the air.

"Ah, well, who knows what the future may hold," Peter murmured. "Jane and I hope to have a nursery full, now that we are finally started."

"You will both be wonderful parents, I'm sure," Susannah assured him, a smile on her face. She slanted a glance at her other companion, walking stony-faced on the other side, before adding, "Just as Mr. Danvers is a wonderful parent. His sons adore him."

He made no acknowledgment of her compliment. After a moment, however, he said, "But they have no mother."

Susannah remained silent, but Peter said, "That is easily remedied, Nick, as Jane has been trying to tell you."

"Not easily, I think. Most women do not care for country life. They want parties, constant admiration, elegant wardrobes. They would not want to be bothered with two grubby schoolboys, or life in the north country."

Both men's eyes were trained on their female companion, but Susannah stared straight ahead, saying nothing.

"I think you have a warped view of females because of your marriage, Nick. Don't you agree, Susannah?" Lord Arbor asked.

"I did not know Mrs. Danvers, my lord."

A long silence followed her response, and Susannah longed to withdraw to the stuffiness of the house, to escape the delicate probing, the stares, the building tension. Nicholas's life, now or in the future, could not concern her. She and Cassie would soon be leaving his home, leaving the joy and warmth, the care and strength he and his staff had given them.

"Is anything wrong, Susannah?" Lord Arbor asked, seeing her distress.

"Nay, my lord. All is well. But I think I am growing chilled. I believe I should return to the house now."

Nicholas Danvers, too, had seen her distress without understanding it. But he could allow her request. "Your wish is our command, right, Peter?" Without another word, he reversed his direction and offered his arm to Susannah. After only a moment's hesitation, she accepted his guidance.

They did not speak until they reached the house again, much to Susannah's relief. She did not want to converse with her employer anymore. In fact, she hoped to avoid him until she had fully planned her course of action. But the determination in his face as he escorted her told her it would be difficult.

Before she could go inside, Nicholas lifted her hand from his arm and carried it to his lips. His unexpected action startled her, and her breathing accelerated as she slowly raised her gaze to his.

"Susannah, I—"

"Mr. Danvers? Mr. Danvers, sir, Mr. Clumpus needs to speak to you, urgent like," a groom said from the path leading to the stable.

Clumpus was his gamekeeper and had served Nicholas faithfully for many years. Even so, he was torn between attending to his duties and staying with the beautiful woman playing havoc with his senses. Finally duty won out, and he stepped back. "I must speak with you later, Susannah."

"Of course, sir," she quietly agreed, vowing to avoid him at all costs. Without waiting for him to demand a particular time for their speaking, she hurried into the house.

Nicholas watched her until she entered the house before turning back to the stable.

"Shall I accompany you, Nick?" Lord Arbor asked.

"No, go enjoy your breakfast. I shall join you short-ly." He strode toward the stables. "Clumpus? Where are you?" he shouted as he entered.

"Here, sir," a wiry little man called.

"What is the matter?"

"I thought I should tell you that I think a trespasser has been making free with your property." A wor-ried frown was on the man's weather-worn face.

Nicholas frowned, also. "There have been poachers before, Clumpus. Why the urgency now?"

"'Tis not a poacher, sir. A man has been spotted about the place, though I've found no signs of poaching. But 'tis not someone passing through. He's been around almost a week now." Rubbing his nose, a sign that Clumpus was thinking, he added, "I can't figure what he's about."

A sense of impending doom filled Nicholas. "Ride out and see if you can find him. If you do, bring him back to me for questioning."

The little man nodded and turned to resaddle his mount. Nicholas added, "And, Clumpus, take sever-al stablehands with you."

As he turned toward the house, Nicholas was in deep thought. He'd never been an advocate of the poaching laws. Game was plentiful in their area, and it supplemented the meager wages some people earned. Clumpus understood his master's philoso-phy and turned a blind eye to occasional poachings on the squire's land.

If Clumpus thought something was unusual about the stranger's presence, Nicholas knew better than to dismiss his suspicions. And he couldn't help but connect the strange words his governess uttered the night before with the sudden appearance of a stranger in the nearest town and now on his own land.

She must be in danger, but had he increased it by forcing her to go into Bloomfield and to attend the party? His hands clenched as he considered the possibility of anyone hurting Susannah.

Until she chose to leave, she was his to protect, and he would do so, he promised himself. Nothing would harm her while she lived in his house. And he refused even to think of her leaving.

11

Susannah hurried into the house, thankful to have escaped Nicholas's scrutiny. She sped past the breakfast room, much to Pritchard's surprise, and didn't stop until she reached her chamber.

"Something be wrong?" Evie asked, looking up from tending the fire.

"No! No, nothing. I just wondered if you would mind bringing me a pot of tea, Evie, and perhaps a slice of Cook's bread."

"Certainly, mum." Evie was surprised. Normally the governess refused to be waited on. She scurried off to prepare a tray.

Susannah sank down on the edge of her bed. Her morning walk had provided exercise, but not the peace she needed, nor the opportunity to plan for her and Cassie's future. A cry from the cradle distracted her from her thoughts.

"Good morning, sweetest. Are you as restless as your mother?" She leaned down and picked up her child, cuddling Cassie against her breasts. The baby settled against her mother and happily drifted off to sleep again.

Susannah considered restoring her to the cradle, but she couldn't resist the comfort her child gave her. Her warmth and contentment restored Susannah's balance.

It also reminded Susannah why she must flee from their lovely home. Cassandra must be protected at all costs. No matter what kind of marriage Susannah had had, Cassandra had a right to her heritage. Susannah must return to London and consult her man of business. After all, she would need more funds if they were to travel to America. And she would need to establish a way to communicate with him about future funds.

Probably she should have done so when she was last in London, but she had been too frightened to trust anyone. Like a fox pursued by hounds, she had only thought to find a safe hiding place. She now realized there was no place safe enough.

If she returned to London immediately, she might discover the information she needed before Gerald could even arrive here, if that was his intent. At least he would not expect her to go closer to him. A shiver ran over Susannah. Although she'd contemplated this before, wasn't she brave enough to take that risk?

She looked down at the child sleeping safely in her arms. Should she leave Cassandra here, in Evie's care, until she consulted with Mr. Amos, her man of business?

After laying the baby gently down in the cradle, Susannah stood over it, staring down at her, while she debated her choices. She would be less noticeable without her child, and the baby would be more comfortable here at the squire's home. But would she be safer, especially if Gerald *was* on his way here? Could Nicholas protect Cassie?

Only if he knew what was happening.

Should she tell him the truth? Susannah paced around the room, confusion making every decision difficult. She had finally concluded that she could trust Nicholas Danvers to protect her child without revealing the entire story when Evie entered the room with a heavily laden tray.

"This reminds me of that first evening you was here," Evie said with a smile.

The maid set the tray down on a table in front of the fire and stood. "I'll just go tidy up the schoolroom."

"Wait, Evie." Susannah stood across the room, staring at the young girl. "Evie, if I—that is, I may have to go away for a few days. Will you look after Cassandra for me?"

"Why, o'course I will. Do you think she's old enough for cow's milk? If not, my ma knows a wet nurse who could come."

"Heavens, I hadn't thought of that." Susannah wondered if she was losing her mind to forget that she nursed her own child. "I—I don't know. Perhaps we should consult the doctor."

"Want me to have Pritchard summon him?"

"Yes, I suppose so. But, Evie . . ." Susannah paused, unsure how to phrase her request. "Perhaps he is visiting Lady Arbor soon?"

"No. Her maid said she was a-waitin' to see her own doctor when they returned home."

"Oh."

"You don't want anyone to know you're seein' the doctor?" The maid looked at her anxiously. "Be there anything wrong?"

"No, of course not. But I haven't told Mr. Danvers that I must go away for a few days and—"

"I'll ask Mr. Pritchard to keep it quiet like. He'll understand," Evie assured her, awkwardly patting her shoulder.

"Thank you, Evie."

"Now, you eat your tea, and I'll have a word with Mr. Pritchard before I go to the schoolroom."

Susannah sat down in front of the tray but couldn't bring herself to actually eat anything. If she was this discomposed talking to Evie, what would she be like when she had to face Nicholas Danvers? His piercing stare would demand honesty, but she couldn't tell him the whole story. No one, not even Nicholas, would believe her. She had no proof. He would think her a foolish female, given to fantastic nightmares.

Finally she poured herself a cup of tea and nibbled on the bread. She needed to refresh herself before facing Nicholas.

She had scarcely reached the schoolroom with Cassandra when a footman requested her to go to the library by Nicholas's request. Even Mrs. Colley noticed her uneasiness. Patting Susannah's shoulder comfortingly, she murmured, "Here now, my dear, the boy's no demon. He'll not harm you."

Susannah managed a half smile for the concerned faces and surrendered her baby to the old lady. With a mumbled promise to return in a few moments, she slowly left the room.

After knocking on the library door, she shook when she heard his voice, ordering her to enter.

Taking a deep breath, she slipped into the room, closing the door behind her.

The squire was standing across the room by a window, his back to her. His powerful frame stood out in relief from the light of the window, his dark hair vibrant and shining. Slowly he turned around to face her. "Susannah. Finally we will have the opportunity to talk."

She was somehow surprised that he was using her first name. His request earlier that morning had only seemed a ploy to keep up with his brother-in-law. "Yes, sir?"

"Sit down." He moved from the window and gestured to the sofa against one wall. She gingerly took a seat on its edge but almost jumped up again when he sat down beside her. With a frown he reached out a big hand to cover hers, tightly clenched in her lap. "I only want to help you, Susannah. Will you explain to me what is wrong?"

"There is nothing you can do."

"You said that last night, but you added the word *murder*." He paused, his eyes never leaving her face, but she couldn't look at him. "I think you should explain what you meant."

"I should not have said that," she muttered. She stared down at his hand, its strength and warmth comforting even though she truly believed he could do nothing to help her.

"But you did." His other hand came under her chin to turn her face toward him. "I have always known you were not here just to find a position. You have been hiding from something. But I did not think it so serious as murder."

His was such a kind face, Susannah thought, as
well as handsome. She had seen him laugh with his
children, show compassion to those in misery, and
she'd thought she'd even seen desire in his eyes as
he'd looked at her on occasion. She found herself
leaning toward him and jumped back, jerking from
his hold.

"Mr. Danvers, I cannot—"

"Do you think you could call me Nicholas? It only
seems fair since I am making free use of your name."
A whimsical smile on his lips distracted her.

"Of course, Mr. Danvers, but—"

"Nicholas," he reminded her, still smiling.

She stared at him, confused. Why was he harping
on her using his name when more important things
were still to be discussed?

"Susannah, we must come to terms with whatever is frightening you. I promise to protect you and
Cassandra if you will just tell me the truth." He took
one of her hands back in his grasp and raised it to
his lips.

"I have told you—"

"You have not told me the truth," he said, the softness leaving his voice. His polite approach hadn't
worked, so he forced himself to be stern. He lowered
her hand from his lips but kept hold of it. "Peter
remembers you from London. He says you are an
heiress."

"I told you I had some money," she said stubbornly, her chin rising.

"So you did. You also told me your husband was
a soldier."

Looking directly into his concerned brown eyes
she said, "That was a lie."

"You also told me you were a widow."

There was a curious stillness in the man next to her as he waited for her answer. "That was not a lie," she whispered. "My husband died before Cassandra was born, but of a hunting accident, not on the Continent."

Nicholas Danvers felt a weight lifted from his shoulders, though he staunchly denied the relief that filled him. He studied her beautiful face even as he asked, "An accident, not murder?"

Surprise marked her face as she looked up at him. "Oh, no, I'm sure it was an accident. My husband was a terrible rider, but he thought himself top of the trees. He insisted on riding a brute of a stallion that he couldn't control."

"Did you love him?"

A curious question for him to ask, Susannah thought, but she answered honestly, "No. At the time of our marriage I thought I might come to love him, but no, I did not. My aunt was so pleased with the match and so convinced it was right for me that I accepted her belief."

"Then, if your husband died in a hunting accident, from whom are you hiding?"

Susannah jumped up, anxious to remove herself from such close quarters. "Mr.—N-Nicholas," she changed after a reproving look, "I cannot tell you what I fear. Perhaps it is a figment of my imagination." She avoided his gaze, taking several more steps away from him, twisting her hands together in front of her.

"Imaginary dragons are easier to slay than real ones, I would think. I am at your service." There was a humorous light to his words that made Susannah even more determined than ever to keep silent.

"I need to go away for a few days."

Her quiet words stirred Nicholas to action. He leapt from the sofa and clasped her arm. "No! You can't—that is, if there is any danger, you would be exposing yourself to it."

"There is something I must do," she whispered before her teeth sank into her bottom lip.

"I will escort you to wherever you are going." He pulled her around to face him. "Susannah, look at me. I will not allow you to leave alone."

Gathering her courage, she raised her chin, her blue-eyed gaze meeting his. "Nicholas, you have no right to hold me here."

He knew she was right, but he was not willing to admit it. "No right? I am your employer. I refuse to allow you to leave your post."

Ducking her head to hide the tears that were in her eyes, she shook her head and whispered, "Then I must resign."

Those words hung in the air between them. Nicholas had long ago decided that Mrs. Brown would not be long in his schoolroom, but now that the moment had come, he could not accept it.

"Susannah," he whispered and drew her into his arms, holding her warmth against him, breathing in her fresh scent, her softness. "Susannah, I must keep you safe. I know that you will leave me, but it must only be when I know you will not be harmed."

She rested her head against his hard chest, the steady thump of his heart soothing to her fears. In spite of propriety that said she should protest his behavior, she felt such peace in those strong arms wrapped about her. But there was also a delicious excitement about his closeness that was like nothing she'd ever experienced.

As if in a dream, she felt his fingers tugging her chin toward him and his lips coming to meet hers. Their firm, cool touch turned to fire as they molded to hers. Her arms stole up to his broad shoulders as the world flew away and only his touch remained.

Nicholas could not remember when a kiss had been so all-powerful, so consuming. When at last he lifted his head, he reveled in her beauty, studying her face as her eyes remained closed and a soft smile dressed her lips. Just as he started to kiss her again, however, those eyes sprang open and reality returned.

"Nicholas!" she protested, pushing her way out of his arms.

"Susannah, I apologize. I did not mean to take advantage of your situation." When she did not run from the room, he continued, "But you must promise you will not set out on your own."

She backed away from him, embarrassed. He must think her a wanton woman to accept his caresses so easily. She was scarcely aware of his words as she fought to suppress the desire to return to his arms.

"Promise me, Susannah."

"What?"

"Promise me that you will not set out on your own. Not yet. Give me the opportunity to protect you."

The determination in his voice told her he would watch her every movement, making escape difficult, unless she lulled him with compliance.

"Very well. I—I will not leave just yet." She edged her way toward the door, eager to escape the temptation he presented.

"You must tell me what you fear, Susannah. How can I help you if you do not?"

"I cannot!" she replied, moving still closer to the door. Escape was almost within her reach in the form of the door when he asked one last question.

"Will you at least tell me your real name?"

Susannah looked at him again. The warmth of his regard reminded her of their embrace. "I am the dowager Lady Craven."

"Craven?" he questioned sharply. "Gerald? You were married to Gerald?"

She paled at his words. He knew her brother-in-law! Thank God she had not told him her suspicions. "No, he is the present Lord Craven, my brother-in-law."

"That's right, he had an older brother who inherited the title."

"H-he is a friend of yours?"

"No. We were at Harrow together."

His eyes seemed to swallow her whole, distracting Susannah from his words but reminding her of her need to escape his presence. "I must return to the schoolroom." Without waiting for a response, she opened the door and ran to the stairs that led to safety.

It took Nicholas half an hour to compose himself. The desire that had filled him when he'd held Susannah in his arms told him how dangerously far he had come in his regard for his governess. He had vowed not to be hurt by another beautiful woman, but he knew it was too late to think he could keep that promise.

Even so, he must offer any assistance he could to her if she truly was in danger. As a gentleman, it was his duty. As a man in love, it was his privilege. Even if that love was not returned.

Finally he left the library and went in search of his brother-in-law. Peter had been in town much more recently than he and would have a better knowledge of what was going on.

He discovered him in the morning room with his wife, studying a sheet of paper.

"Well, I think Letitia a lovely name, Peter. Why don't you like it?" Jane looked up as he entered. "What do you think, Nicholas?"

"About what?" he asked, his thoughts still with Susannah.

"The name Letitia. We are discussing names for the baby. Peter, of course, is sure it will be a boy, but I think we should pick out a girl's name, also. Don't you think so?"

"Of course, Jane, that's a lovely name. Uh, Peter, could I interrupt you for a few words?"

"Of course, Nicholas, what is the matter? Do you need my opinion about what to plant in the meadow?" Peter asked with a smile. He and his brother-in-law had frequent arguments about farming methods, neither convincing the other but both enjoying the banter.

When his attempt at humor passed unnoticed by Nicholas, Peter stood. "Is aught the matter?"

"No, of course not," Nicholas assured him, a sideways glance at his sister, who was now watching him closely.

"What do you want to talk to Peter about?" she asked, sitting up from the chaise longue where she'd been resting.

"An estate matter. I just wanted his opinion." Nicholas was having difficulty concentrating on his sister's questions when all he could think about was Susannah.

She turned her head sideways and stared at her brother. "I just requested a tea tray. Why not join us and you can ask him when we refresh ourselves."

Nicholas looked at Jane blankly, at a loss for a reason to speak to Peter alone, but Peter came to his aid. "Darling, I don't think you would enjoy a discussion about crops. Why don't you ask Susannah to come down from the schoolroom and have tea with you while we repair to the library?"

"But, Peter, we haven't settled on any names."

He walked over to her side and kissed her brow. "But we still have six months to make up our minds. Besides, I suspect Susannah will be of great help in choosing names. You and she could narrow the list, and then I'll be better able to make my choice." He caressed her cheek lovingly, and she smiled up at him. Nicholas watched them with envious eyes.

"Very well. But you must promise not to be gone too long."

"Never, my love. Nick, ring the bell for Pritchard, will you?" Peter requested. "And you might ask him for tea for us in the library. I was counting on having a few coconut macaroons with my cup of tea."

Nicholas did as he was told, but he was irritated by all the details required to spring his brother-in-law from Jane's grasp. When Pritchard arrived and was given instructions, Peter was finally free to leave

Jane to await Susannah's arrival.

When the door was closed behind them, Peter clutched Nicholas's arm with a frown on his face that told Nicholas he had been playacting for his wife's comfort. "What is the matter?"

12

Nicholas only shook his head and gestured toward the library. When they had entered that room and closed the door behind them, he explained his difficulty.

"I have discovered Susannah's real name, but not the problem from which she hides. However, I thought you might know something when you heard the name."

Impatiently Peter said, "Well, what is it, Nick?"

"Lady Craven."

"Yes, of course," Peter said, nodding in agreement. "She married Reginald Craven. I remember now. It seemed a shame. She was so bright and beautiful, and he did not have a good reputation."

"Are you also familiar with the new Lord Craven, Gerald?" Nicholas watched him carefully to see his reaction.

"Good lord. I had forgotten about him. He's a thoroughly nasty piece of work. He even made his brother appear gentlemanly." Something in Nicholas's face made him ask, "Do you know him?"

"We were at school together. At least, we were until he was sent down." Nicholas firmed his lips in distaste. "There was the matter of his attacking a young maid and having his way with her against her will, in a particularly brutal fashion."

"You don't think—"

"I don't know. She would not tell me what she feared. But knowing Gerald, it must be something horrible. Perhaps saw him attack some female, even if it wasn't her. It would be very disturbing to her. Gerald may have found out and threatened her."

"But surely if she left, he would assume she would not report him. Besides, he's a peer of the realm. No one would take her word against his, even if she is the widow of the former earl."

"Then why is she being pursued?"

Peter's head snapped up, and he stared at Nicholas. "Pursued? You mean someone has threatened her here?"

"Not yet. But there's been a stranger in the area for the last week or so. And she must fear pursuit, or she would not have constantly refused to be seen off the estate. That is, until Jane and I forced her."

"Do not blame yourself, Nick," Peter assured him, resting a hand on his shoulder. "You could not have known what harm it would do, if any. After all, nothing has yet happened."

"I went against her wishes. I forced *her* to go against her wishes. Because I could not bear for her to keep her secrets." He turned away from Peter. "Because I could not resist her beauty. I wanted to punish her, I think, for being beautiful."

Peter smiled in sympathy. "She's a lovely lady," he said quietly.

Spinning around, Nicholas agreed. "Yes. And yes, I have succumbed to her beauty, to her sweetness, her gentleness. But I have no hold over her. She will leave when I have ensured her safety."

"You don't know that, Nick. I think she feels something for you, also."

Nicholas waved his hand in dismissal of his brother-in-law's words. "That does not matter. I must keep her safe. I must find a way to protect her, and yet I don't know for sure what the difficulty is."

"Perhaps her man of business might shed some light on the difficulty."

"Possibly, but I don't know who he is, and I do not want to ask her such a question."

"But I know who he is." Peter smiled in amusement at his friend's startled look. "I know. It is highly irregular, but I arrived at my man of business's office one day just as Gerald was leaving. Henry was so disturbed by the interview, he could not hold back his complaints. It seemed he served Gerald as well as his brother and found neither to his taste."

"What is his name? I'll write him at once and send one of my best men to deliver it personally." Even as he spoke, Nicholas moved to his desk, where writing materials could be found.

"Henry Amos. I'll write a note vouching for you, so Henry will have no qualms about answering freely. He might even feel the need to come consult with Lady Craven in person."

"That might be best. Ring for Pritchard," Nicholas said in clipped tones even as he began to write. To have finally found something he could do was a great relief.

Susannah debated over her gown that evening for several minutes. The brown wool was detestable, but she did not want to appear to be dressing to—to attract attention. She would have had dinner in her room if she hadn't thought Nicholas would come up the stairs himself to see why she was avoiding him.

However, she did finally choose the Bishop's blue muslin, but only because she couldn't bear to wear the brown wool again, she assured herself. If she were staying, she could order several more gowns.

If she were staying, she would be content and happy. Even if Nicholas only let her stay as the governess. To have Theodore and Edward under her care, and a safe, happy place for Cassandra, and to be able to see Nicholas, that would be enough.

If she were staying.

Pushing away her thoughts and the tears that threatened to spill from her eyes, Susannah finished dressing and attended to her hair before Evie could arrive to do so. A simple braided coronet was easy enough. Just as she put the last pin in place, Evie entered the room.

"Why, Mrs. Brown, you've already finished your hair. I hurried from the schoolroom to do it for you."

"That's all right, Evie. After all, this is not a special evening." She stood and turned around for her maid's inspection. "Is all in order?"

"Course it 'tis. You look pretty as a picture."

"Thank you, Evie. You will remain here with Cassandra until I return, won't you? You won't leave her alone?"

"Not if you don't want me to. Is she sickening for something?" The maid tiptoed over to the cradle to look at the sleeping infant.

"She did seem a little warm when I fed her," Susannah lied, not wanting to alarm Evie with her fears.

"I'll take good care of her. I've already had my dinner, so I'll stay right here beside her till you return."

"Thank you, Evie," Susannah whispered as she left the room, praying that she was right in her thinking she had a few more days of safety.

When she reached the parlor door, she paused to straighten her shoulders and gather her courage.

"The others are waiting, Mrs. Brown," Pritchard said, smiling as he reached around her and opened the doors.

His sudden appearance startled her, leaving her no choice but to enter. She looked cautiously at Nicholas, suddenly uncertain of what she should say or do. The intensity of his dark eyes was almost unbearable. "Good evening. I hope I am not late."

"Not at all," Jane assured her. "You must come support my choice of names. Peter does not care for Thessalonica."

"I'll not have my child named after a country!"

"But it has such a pretty sound to it," Jane protested. When Peter appeared to remain firm in his opinion, she said, "Well, perhaps we should name her Susannah, in honor of all the assistance Susannah has given me."

"Oh, no, I—"

"Perhaps you should first determine if that is her true name." Nicholas's words came out unduly harsh, and he let out a low groan, regretting the

comment immediately. Susannah's face paled, and
she looked as if she might faint. Jane turned bewildered eyes upon him.

"Whatever do you mean, Nick?" she demanded.

"My apologies, Susannah. I spoke without thinking." He wanted to go to her, comfort her, and say
how sorry he was, but instead he remained silent.

Susannah sank down onto the nearest chair,
unsure of how to explain. "I suppose I deserve
such censure, Mr. Danvers, since I lied about
my name. But my true name *is* Susannah . . .
Covington, before my marriage."

"I was not attempting to censure you. I just—I
wanted to know your name." The desire to hold her
in his arms again was overwhelming. Her beauty
was as vibrant as ever, but it was her sadness that
touched him.

"But of course you would not use your unmarried
name. What is Nicholas raving about?" Jane asked,
confused.

Susannah explained, "I'm afraid my name is not
Brown, my lady. It is Lady Craven. The dowager
Lady Craven. I am truly a widow, but—"

"Lady Craven? Peter, did you hear? Susannah is
titled! But what are you doing here, as a governess? Surely you are not poverty-stricken?" Even
more confused than before, Jane looked at the
other three occupants in the room to enlight-
en her.

Lord Arbor moved to his wife's side. "My dear,
I don't think we should ask Susannah such person-
al questions. Is it all right if we continue to call you
Susannah?"

"Of course, my lord."

"Then you must call me Peter." His calm smile earned him one in return and spawned jealousy in Nicholas's heart.

"Thank you, Peter."

Before Jane could express her amazement at such a turn of events, Pritchard announced dinner.

Susannah was not surprised to discover the squire awaiting her arrival in the stableyard the next morning. She *was* surprised, however, to find several other horsemen apparently waiting for her.

"Good morning, Susannah," Nicholas called as she came into sight. "Do you mind if Clumpus, my gamekeeper, and several of his underlings ride with us partway this morning? I want to show him something in the north pasture."

"Of course not, Mr. Danvers, but there is no need for me to accompany you. I can ride alone."

Nicholas's face grew stern and he ordered crisply, "You are never to ride out alone, Susannah. I have given orders that you must be accompanied by a groom if Peter or myself is not available."

"But, Nicholas—"

"Mount up. We are waiting."

She did not appreciate his abrupt manner, but to argue in front of the other men would not be appropriate. She vowed to take up the matter with him once they were alone.

For the better part of an hour, though Nicholas rode at her side, he confined his conversation to his gamekeeper. Several times they paused for the man to give orders to one of the other horsemen, who then left their group, before they continued on.

They had reached the north pasture when they paused a final time, and Clumpus and the one remaining rider left them. Susannah watched the two horsemen disappear into the surrounding woods, saying nothing.

"I apologize for not being better company, Susannah," Nicholas murmured, but she did not look his way.

"It is nothing, sir."

"Shall we give our mounts some real exercise now?"

Never able to resist a good gallop, Susannah looked at him out of the corner of her eye and then nodded. He swung his mount back in the direction they had come, holding the bay back to be sure Susannah followed his lead.

Once they were both facing in the direction of the manor house, he urged his horse forward and she did likewise, not slowing down until they topped the hill a quarter of a mile above the house.

"Exercise does clear the cobwebs, does it not?" he said, admiring the green pastures of his estate.

"Yes," Susannah agreed, her eyes hungrily tracing his figure as he majestically sat his horse. She didn't have much longer to enjoy such outings.

Turning back toward her, he said, "Susannah, I apologize for my manner at the beginning of our ride. It was awkward to explain the difficulty with such an audience." He leaned forward slightly as he studied her face.

"There is no audience now."

"No. Well, it is just that I did not take your fears seriously until the evening of our soiree. I apologize for not doing so. Now I will take all the precautions

possible. So, I request that you never ride out alone."
He knew one word about the stranger would convince her more than what he had just said. But he
did not want to unduly alarm her.

Susannah met his gaze for the first time that morning, and she knew she would never be able to resist
that look of concern, of caring. A look her husband
had never given her. "Very well," she agreed.

With a warm smile he raised his hand to run a
knuckle down her soft cheek. "Thank you. I will
keep my promise to protect you."

"I am not your responsibility, Mr. Danvers."

"Nicholas."

She'd begun thinking of him as Nicholas, but
her rapid breathing and racing heart told her she
needed more distance than he was allowing her.
She could not give in to her desires and put either
him or his children in danger.

Suddenly her impatient chestnut mare jerked forward a few steps, breaking the spell he had cast.
"Thank you for your concern, Nicholas, but I
would not have you make sacrifices for me. If—
if I am right, it is even possible that you might be
injured or—"

Urging his bay stallion closer to her mare, he
pressed his leg against her slim thigh and slipped
his hand beneath the coil of auburn hair at the nape
of her neck that was gloriously shining in the early
morning sun. "There will be no sacrifice, Susannah.
I will not allow it."

Being so close to Nicholas, she could feel the pow-
er of his strength and desire—and love? But the viv-
id and clear memory of her maid's rigid form sent a
shudder up her spine that racked her body, and she

knew she could not put him, or his children, in jeopardy.

"Never fear, sweetheart," he whispered before his lips covered hers. Although his behavior was reprehensible and improper, his feelings, long repressed, surged out of control as he longed to reassure her.

The kiss began as comfort, which Susannah sorely needed, but her lips moved over his with a wanting that shook her to the core. Her marital duties had been performed adequately, witness Cassandra, but she had never felt hunger, need for a man, as she felt for Nicholas. To be in his arms, to let him protect her as he wished, was a tantalizing glimpse of a happier place than she'd ever known.

Nicholas drew back reluctantly, afraid if he lingered longer, he would tumble her to the ground to finish what was rapidly becoming a passionate embrace. His hand still caressed her neck as he gathered himself to offer an apology, a hollow one admittedly, for his behavior.

Susannah, however, did not wait for his words, whatever they might be. With tears forming in her beautiful blue eyes and a tragic look on her face, she jerked from his touch and set her mount at a breakneck pace down the hill.

In spite of his stallion's protest, Nicholas did not follow. With misery in his heart he watched her until she reached the stableyard safely, all the while cursing himself under his breath.

She was a gently bred woman, unused to men's baser natures, he told himself. Though she was a widow, it was clear her marriage had been less than happy. Probably her husband had lain with her only a few times and, once she was increasing, had sought his pleasures elsewhere. A groan welled up within him. He could not imagine ever looking at another woman, much less wanting to touch one, if he had Susannah at his side.

He lost himself in the daydream of waking beside her each morning, her auburn locks a dark shadow on the white pillow, as she caressed him with warmth and tenderness, all of her love directed toward him rather than his children. The hunger that filled him from his dreams could never be assuaged with the food from Cook's kitchen. Only with Susannah.

He had thought himself insulated from the pain he now suffered. A promise to ignore the distaff side of life had been easily kept until a brave-hearted beauty had invaded his kingdom. Without even trying to seduce him, she'd stolen his heart away.

Straightening his shoulders, he moved his horse forward, slowly down the hill. In spite of his dreams, his wants, his needs, he must stand aside. Susannah had not asked for his mauling of her and had run from him at the first opportunity. Until this mystery was solved, Nicholas vowed to watch over Susannah, but when all was well again, he also promised himself to step aside if she chose to leave, as any gentleman should do. But he wouldn't do it because he was proper and well bred; he would do it because he loved her and he didn't want to deny her her proper place in society as a wealthy, titled beauty. He doubted his lifestyle would ever be enough for any woman—especially Susannah. After all, the country was only her hiding place.

*   *   *

Susannah childishly hid in her chamber after her early morning ride, thankful that she'd already nursed Cassandra and let Evie take her to the nursery. Lying on her bed, she touched her hands to her cheeks, which were still aflame with color at her wanton behavior. Nicholas Danvers had always had a poor opinion of women, and now she had only confirmed his belief.

How could she have so forgotten herself as to cling to his broad shoulders, to mold her lips to his?

Even as she thought of their embrace, a delicious heat rose within her. Had he not withdrawn, probably in disgust at her behavior, she would have allowed her passion to overcome all reason. Only briefly did she let herself think of where that passion could have led them. She knew it would be different with Nicholas than with her husband, but her inexperience could not tell her how much. A frustrated groan rose within her, shaming her even more.

Forcing her thoughts away from Nicholas, she abruptly sat up and jumped from the bed and splashed cold water on her pink cheeks. Cassie's safety had to be foremost in her mind and the real danger she faced demanded her attention. Not the dangerous attraction of the handsome man she'd left on the hilltop.

13

Susannah took pains to avoid her employer, seeing him only briefly, and never alone, for the next several days. Such behavior did not take a great deal of thought or effort, since he appeared to be avoiding her, also. Sure that he condemned her behavior, Susannah was not surprised.

Though she kept herself busy in the schoolroom and acting as companion to Jane, her mind raced with the question of what her next move should be. She finally decided against leaving Cassandra behind, realizing it would endanger both her and the baby if she returned. Time was running out.

Only two things happened to disturb the peace of the manor house. First, Susannah had forgotten her request for Evie to send for the doctor. When Dr. Grimes appeared the morning of her last ride with Nicholas, she apologized for his efforts and offered him payment for his visit.

He refused, saying a cup of tea would be payment enough, as he'd had a long morning. Susannah immediately sent for a tea tray. Unfortunately, as it arrived, Jane, Peter, and Nicholas entered the morning room.

Susannah's cheeks turned bright red as Nicholas avoided her eyes. But his apparent avoidance of her did not keep him from asking the reason for the doctor's visit after everyone had been served.

"Come to pay a visit to my sister?" he asked casually.

"No, I came—"

"At my request. I thought Cassie was running a fever."

Susannah's words drew everyone's attention, including a surprised doctor, but he said nothing to contradict her.

"Is she all right?" Nicholas asked, his brow furrowed. He looked at the doctor for an answer, not Susannah.

"He said it was just the sniffles," she responded, studying the brown liquid in her teacup.

"Yes, it is quite common for babies, you know," Dr. Grimes said calmly.

Susannah sent him a grateful look.

Nicholas intercepted that look, and it chilled his heart. Susannah was lying . . . again. Was she ill herself? Now what was she hiding? As much as he loved her and wanted to help her, her refusal to tell him anything frustrated him beyond belief.

"Well, thank you for the tea, Mrs. Brown. I'll be on my way," the doctor said as he stood, smiling at everyone.

Nicholas escorted Dr. Grimes to the hall, conscious of Susannah's blue eyes following the two of them even as he closed the door to the morning room.

"She did not call you to look at her child, did she?" he asked tersely.

Dr. Grimes hesitated before answering, unsure where his loyalties should lie. "No, sir."

"Why did she request you to call?"

Dr. Grimes was too young to have escorted Nicholas Danvers into the world, but he had done so for Nicholas's children and was not intimidated by his manner. Raising one eyebrow, he said, "If I had seen anyone, it would not be right to tell you of the results of my examination, you know, unless, of course, it affected their employment."

"Why?" Nicholas simply repeated.

"I don't know. She told me my services were no longer necessary." With an apologetic smile, Dr. Grimes took his hat from Pritchard, waiting at his side, then nodded his head and left.

Nicholas stood still, trying to understand her reasons, when Peter joined him.

"Is anything amiss?"

"Damn it, I don't know! The woman keeps her own counsel, and it is driving me insane."

Peter placed a sympathetic hand on his shoulder. "Come to the library. I will let you win an argument about planting oats again this year. That will cheer you up."

He was wrong, Nicholas thought wearily, but at least it would prove a distraction.

Jane caused the second disruption of their quiet existence the next day while the four of them were enjoying an afternoon tea.

"Peter, I told Nancy to start packing first thing tomorrow morning. It should not take her longer than one day, so we can leave the day after tomorrow."

"No!" Both men exploded with the same word, causing the ladies to stare.

Neither elaborated on their protest, nor did they look at the surprised women.

"What are you talking about?" Jane demanded. "I admit I will be sorry to take leave of Nicholas and Susannah, but I have much to do in preparation for our child. You know, I will soon be too . . . too tired to accomplish many tasks," she added, embarrassed to mention that it would be her changing body rather than her energy that would limit her activities.

"My dear," Peter said, "surely there is no hurry. I thought you would enjoy visiting with Susannah a little longer."

"Certainly I enjoy Susannah's company, Peter, but—"

"Peter and I are working on a new kind of oat, Jane," Nicholas said, interrupting her. "We have a small wager on the result. I would appreciate it if you could delay your departure just a few days more. Peter would never accept his losses if he did not see the result in person." Nicholas smiled endearingly at his sister.

Susannah, however, as little as she'd looked at him in the past several days, saw something in his eyes that rang false. Whatever had caused his and Peter's rejection of Jane's plans, it was more serious than a wager.

"You have planted oats already?" Jane asked. Although it was April and southern England had been warmed by the spring sun, the north still suffered chilly evenings.

The two men exchanged a brief, indecipherable look. Jane and Susannah waited patiently for their answer.

"Only a small patch in a sheltered pasture," Nicholas assured Jane, but he avoided her eyes.

"Well, I suppose we may delay our departure for a week, but no later." Jane looked at her husband. "Will that do?"

"I hope so, my love. I would not want to disappoint you," he assured her, a tender smile on his lips.

Susannah envied their intimate warmth and was irresistibly drawn to Nicholas's face. Their gazes collided, and each looked away quickly. He could not even bear to look at her, she told herself, her eyes burning with unshed tears. Weakness did not become her, so she gathered her strength, stood up, and walked to the bookcase, pretending to choose another book to read.

Nicholas let his eyes slowly return to Susannah since her back was to him and he could admire her without notice or embarrassment. He missed the ease with which they had once talked, and he cursed his desire that had made her uncomfortable with him. Determined to find a way to regain her trust, he allowed her withdrawal and turned to his sister instead.

"Well, I am glad that is settled, Jane. It is kind of you to tolerate our experiment."

"I would extract a favor from you, Nicholas, in return," she replied, a speculative look in her eye that alarmed her brother. He'd seen it before.

"What favor?"

"That is not a gentlemanly response, Nick. You are supposed to say my wish is your command. Is that not so, Susannah?"

Appealed to, Susannah turned to face Jane, a book opened in her hand. "Yes, of course."

"You see?" Jane crowed triumphantly to Nicholas. "Susannah agrees. What will she think of you if you do not comply with my request?"

"No worse than she does now, I assure you," Nicholas responded cryptically, and was rewarded by a brief flash of Susannah's blue eyes before she returned her attention to her book. "Besides, she hasn't known you as long as I have."

"Well, this time it is nothing so very onerous. I only want you to promise to bring Susannah, yes, and Cassandra, Theodore, and Edward, too, to visit me when I am at home, unable to be out and about. It would relieve my boredom." Jane watched her brother, waiting for his agreement.

"A promise easily made, my dear," he assured her with a smile. "I want your time to be a happy one, and we would enjoy the visit, wouldn't we, Susannah?"

Susannah lifted her head to agree quietly before placing the book back on the shelf and returning to the sofa. She sipped her tea slowly, glancing about the room, realizing that she would never have the joy of being a part of a large family. She would never share in their easy banter and humor. But Cassandra would be more than enough to fill her life, she assured herself. As long as she could protect her child from Gerald.

*   *   *

Susannah's plans were formulated, and she intended to put them into effect the next evening, after everyone had gone to bed. But during the day she had to face the people she loved and pretend everything was normal.

However, she did not go down to breakfast, nor for a morning ride. She could not face Nicholas. When word came to the schoolroom in the form of Jane that the men would not be returning to the house for luncheon, she was relieved as well as disappointed.

Desperate for a distraction, she suggested a picnic to Jane, accompanied by the two boys. Edward and Theodore immediately voiced their enthusiasm, and Jane agreed.

"I might as well ride while I can. It won't be long before it will be impossible," she said.

"Wonderful. Evie, go to the kitchen and ask Cook if she will prepare us a picnic luncheon. I will speak to Colley for a moment, Jane, if you will keep an eye on these two. They are supposed to be practicing their penmanship."

"Aha! I will crack the whip over their heads. They'll be perfect by the time you return," Jane assured her with a laugh, adding a ridiculous frown for her nephews' benefit.

Amid their laughter, Susannah slipped into the nursery to explain their plans to the old nurse.

Soon they were all mounted and riding slowly across the nearest meadow, accompanied by several grooms. Though Susannah had protested their presence, since she was not alone, the head stableman had insisted.

"Though, of course, I have no complaints about having someone around to wait on me, I do not understand Nicholas's insistence," Jane complained as they rode along.

"He is probably afraid you and I could not handle the horses should there be an accident."

Jane looked at her sharply. "Susannah, you are a better horsewoman than I. My brother said so. And I rode these hills unaccompanied many times. It never occurred to him then to forbid such activity."

"You were not increasing then, I hope," Susannah teased, hoping to distract her friend.

With a surprised look on her face, Jane laughed. "I had forgotten. Is that not bizarre?"

"No," Susannah said softly. "There were times it was difficult for me to believe I was having a baby, even when I was great with child."

"You did not have a happy marriage, did you?" Jane asked, her famous directness not curbed by the children's presence.

Susannah stared straight ahead over her horse's ears for several minutes before answering. "No. But I suppose my marriage was not unusual. I think yours and Peter's is the unusual marriage."

"Unfortunately it is true. My friends stare at us when we dance with each other, or I complain of his absence. They are constantly in search of their next flirtation." A troubled look settled on Jane's face. "Nick's wife was like that. She cared nothing for him, and he, poor darling, wore his heart on his sleeve."

"He loved her?"

"Yes, for at least a month after their marriage. She kept her indifference hidden until the vows

were said. Then she revealed her true self." Jane
looked around to be sure the other riders could not
overhear before adding, "I even think she—she was
unfaithful to him, but you must never say a word
about it."

Her heart aching for the kind, gentle man she
loved, Susannah tried to imagine turning to someone else if Nicholas loved her, and she found it
impossible to even consider. Other men paled in
comparison.

They reached the spot chosen for their picnic
and Susannah began to relax, but it was difficult
to maintain her pose with such heartbreaking
thoughts. Also, this was her last afternoon with
Edward and Theodore, and that in itself was heart-
wrenching enough, without thoughts of their father.
She had come to love the two boys as if they were
her own. To part from them would be difficult.

A pink-and-blue checkered coverlet was spread
on the early spring grass by the time the ladies had
dismounted. One groom took their horses while the
other set about the food.

"I'm starved!" Edward exclaimed, eyeing the
dishes eagerly. However, he didn't forget to offer
his arm as escort to his aunt. With a nudge from his
brother, Theodore did the same for Susannah.

"Thank you, darling," she whispered to the little boy, dropping a kiss on the top of his unruly
brown hair. All four settled around the food and
soon were munching contentedly, while the two
servants moved off to a short distance and began
their meal, also.

Edward, between bites of the quail, launched
into a long tale about Theodore's behavior in the

schoolroom the day before when Susannah had
been having tea with Jane, Peter, and Nicholas. Poor
Theodore, anxious to refute his brother's claims,
leaned forward to protest, in the process dumping
his plate onto the coverlet.

Susannah jumped forward to try to catch the plate.
The loud crack that rang out at the same time froze
her movements.

Jane screamed, and Edward, in the midst of laughter, grew deathly pale. The two menservants sprang
to their feet, one of them yelling to halt fire.

They had been told they were supposed to protect
the ladies, but they hadn't understood how serious
the danger might be. Jane had no idea why a shot
had been fired, and Edward and Theodore were just
as shocked by what had occurred.

Only Susannah was not.

She knew she'd pushed her luck too far.

"Get down!" she commanded the others, putting
herself between them and the direction from which
the shot had come. "Crawl to the horses as quickly as
possible. When you mount, put your horse between
you and the—the gunman. And then ride as fast as
you can. Wait for no one."

"But, Susannah—" Edward protested.

"Obey me, Edward," Susannah ordered with
a voice of steel, one Edward had not heard
before.

The two grooms had advanced in the direction of
the fired shot. Susannah called them back, but they
ignored her.

Running to where the others were mounted, she
whacked the animals on their flanks, sending them

galloping toward home in spite of Edward's protests. As she gathered the reins of the three remaining horses, there was another shot fired and one of the grooms howled with pain. Susannah watched the figure crumple to the ground in the distance.

"Dear Lord, please not another death." She estimated she had time to reach the other two before the gunman had time to reload. She sprang into the saddle and led their horses to them.

"Is he alive?" she demanded, bent low over her saddle.

"Yes'm, I be alive," Jem, the wounded man, answered.

"Help him into the saddle," she told the other groom, Andy. "We must hurry."

Susannah held the horses steady while they mounted, both looking nervously over their shoulders. In only seconds the three of them sped away. Another shot was fired as they rode, but they were too far away for it to do any harm.

After they had ridden for several minutes, Susannah called a halt and examined the man's wound. His arm was bleeding profusely. She tore several strips from her petticoat and bound up the wound without dismounting, hoping to stop the flow of blood. The other man paled at the red liquid. When his face went from white to green, Susannah ordered curtly, "Look away! And hold the horses steady.

"That will have to do for now," she added. "Can you make it to the house?"

Jem valiantly nodded, unable to speak because his teeth were clenched. She looked at Andy, who was hiding his face from her, ashamed of his weakness.

"Come, we'll each ride beside him and keep him in the saddle. But we must hurry."

"Aye," Andy agreed roughly and moved to the other side of his friend.

When they reached the stables a few minutes later, they found a group of horsemen gathered, preparing to come rescue them.

"There they be!" someone shouted as they topped the rise just above the stables. When they met, attention was given to the wounded man.

"He'll need the doctor," Susannah ordered.

Clumpus assisted her down. "He's already been sent for to see Miss Jane," he assured her. "I mean Lady Arbor."

"She is injured?" Susannah asked with a gasp. She hadn't thought the others had been hit.

"No! No, madam. But she's right upset. We just thought, in the circumstances—"

"Yes, you are quite right. Where is Lord Arbor? She will want him beside her."

"They'm rode into Bloomfield. I sent a boy after 'em as soon as the others arrived."

"Thank you, Clumpus. You have done just as you ought."

"Thank *you*, madam. Tim here will see you to the house," the old man said, gesturing to a young stable lad.

Even as she nodded, he turned to mount a horse. "Where are you going?" she asked sharply.

"Why, to find the man who shot at all of you, Mrs. Brown," he explained, a puzzled look on his face.

"No! Do not leave the stableyard!" Her voice was hard and full of command.

"Now, Mrs. Brown, the master would be put out if I didn't pursue him."

"I forbid it!" she repeated, her voice rising as shock set in. "I cannot be responsible for more deaths!"

14

Nicholas and Peter were entering the drive to the manor house when the boy found them. He scarce completed his first words, "Sir, someone shot at the ladies—" before he found himself alone again. The gentlemen had urged their mounts to a dead run, heading toward the stables.

The stablehand immediately set out in pursuit, not intending to be left behind. Therefore, all three were in time to hear Susannah's dramatic cry.

The men exchanged panic-stricken looks before they leapt from their horses.

"Who has died?" Nicholas cried hoarsely even as he shoved his way through to a wide-eyed Susannah.

"No one, sir," Clumpus hastily assured him, relieving both men. "I don't know what the lady meant. We were getting ready to go look for whoever shot at them."

"Where is my wife?" Peter demanded.

"She be in the manor house, my lord," Clumpus added, "Only one of the stablehands was hurt. Lady Arbor and the two lads are safe enough."

"Someone was actually hurt?" Somehow, Nicholas had not believed the danger to be quite so real.

"We sent for the doctor when Lady Arbor and the two boys arrived, sir, so happen he'll be here soon."

Nicholas was unable to make sense of the situation since he couldn't imagine his sister and his children going out without Susannah. He grabbed Susannah's arm and hugged her tightly, but briefly, before handing her stunned form to Peter. "Take Susannah to the house and see about Jane and the boys."

"But—"

"They need you, Peter. Come, Clumpus. Can anyone show us where the shooting occurred?"

"Aye," the other groom, Andy, spoke, moving to Nicholas's side. "I were wi'em."

Though a thousand questions leapt into his mind, Nicholas only said, "Lead the way. Clumpus, are the men armed?"

"Aye, sir."

Without any more discussion, the small band of men headed back toward the picnic spot even as Susannah protested, her sudden scream rising above the pounding of the hooves.

When Peter led a shaken Susannah into the morning room, the three people huddled together on the sofa gave a joyous cry and rushed to hug her.

"We were afraid for you," Jane said through her tears.

The two boys only clung to her, saying nothing, but they refused to turn loose as Peter moved them back to the sofa.

The boys' need for reassurance drew Susannah from her misery, and she gathered them into her arms as she sat down. Peter held Jane tightly against him, vowing never to let her leave his sight again.

The doctor's arrival jolted them from their tears. "Who is hurt?" Dr. Grimes asked as he rushed in. "My lady? The baby?"

"No, no, I don't think so. I was just frightened," Jane said shakily.

"Have you seen Jem?" Susannah demanded, jumping up.

"No, is he injured?"

"He was shot in the arm and was bleeding considerably," she explained. Her words brought a green tinge to Jane's face as well as a moan.

"Have Lady Arbor put to bed at once. I'll look at her as soon as I treat the wound." He turned to leave and found Susannah at his side.

"I'll assist you," she assured him, wiping her face of the tears she'd shed.

"Nay, Mrs. Brown, 'tis not neces—"

"You don't understand!" Susannah cried, cutting him off. "It is my fault Jem has been shot. I *must* help!"

Peter and the doctor exchanged looks, and Peter gave a brief nod. Dr. Grimes took the distraught lady's arm and led her from the room, wondering if he would be required to deal with two patients at once.

"What did she mean?" Jane asked as the door closed behind the others. "Why would the shooting be Susannah's fault?"

"All will come clear soon, my love. Right now we must obey the doctor's orders for you." He looked at the two children, staring forlornly at the door. "Susannah is safe, as is everyone, boys. Go to the nursery and reassure Colley. She may have heard rumors and be alarmed. I'll have Cook send up a treat for you, too."

A sense of purpose helped Edward and Theodore pull themselves together, and everyone left the morning room to follow the various orders given.

No one was found as the men scoured the area. After several hours Nicholas called a halt to the search and led the return home. On the way, he questioned the groom about the events of the day.

"We'd be dead if not for Mrs. Brown, sir." Andy gulped back the fear that rose in him again. "We thought 'twas a careless hunter who didn't see us. When we ran toward him, yelling, he shot Jem."

"Did you run then?"

"Didn't have time. But Mrs. Brown had gotten the others mounted and sent them on. Then she brought our horses to us. We all rode away as fast as we could. He fired one more shot, but we were safe. But if she hadn't come for us, I guess we'd both be dead."

"I'm grateful she had the courage to do so," Nicholas said, but his heart contracted with fear at the risk Susannah had run.

Upon their arrival back at the manor house, they discovered Jem had been tended by the doctor. Though weak, he was comfortable and the center of attention among the servants. Nicholas paused to thank him for his care of his family, just as he'd thanked Andy.

"Me and Andy didn't do much, sir," Jem protested. "It was Mrs. Brown who saved us. She even helped the doctor take out the bullet. And she didn't faint or nothin'."

After leaving Jem to his glory, Nicholas mounted the stairs, his thoughts on Susannah. His wife had never concerned herself with anyone's health, even her children's, unless it affected her own. Susannah amazed him. Her generous heart was greater even than her beauty.

Peter met him at the top of the stairs leading up from the kitchen. "I heard you had returned. Did you find anything?"

"We found the place from which the shots were fired and where his horse was hidden, but nothing more," Nicholas told him with a sigh. He wearily turned toward the stairs leading to the bedchambers. "Is everyone all right?"

"Yes. They are all sleeping now, Nick, even the boys." Peter took him by the arm and led him to the library. "Pritchard, bring some refreshment for the squire."

Pritchard, who had already spoken to those belowstairs, hurried to the kitchen.

Nicholas sank down on the sofa, exhaustion and shock finally overcoming him, and covered his face with his hands before saying, "Dear God, Peter, that was too close a call. The gunman was very near. The men said Susannah jumped forward to keep Teddy from spilling his plate just as the gun was first fired. That is the only reason she is still alive."

"So you think the attack was aimed at Susannah, and not a poacher's bullet gone astray?"

With a sigh Nicholas repeated the story of the afternoon's adventure, explaining Susannah's care of Jane and the boys, and her return for the servants.

"That is why she did not arrive with the others!" Peter exclaimed. "I could not understand why Jane and the boys were out alone." After a moment's silence he added, "You are right. Obviously Susannah was the target. What do we do now?"

"I have been asking myself that very question. First, I am going to send word to all our neighbors to watch for any strangers in the area. Also, the shopkeepers in Bloomfield. And then we are going to keep our family locked up in the house until the man is caught," Nicholas promised, his words as unbendable as steel.

Peter stood and paced across the room. Finally he came back to stand before his brother-in-law. "I think you must insist that Susannah tell us what is going on. She must not put everyone at danger without revealing the reason."

Nicholas stared up at his friend and saw a reflection of his own horror as he realized how close death had come to those he loved. "You are right, Peter. I will force her to tell us first thing in the morning, after she's had a chance to recover from the events of this day."

Instead of resting, Susannah was tearfully composing letters at her writing table. Two brief notes had been written already to Theodore and Edward, telling the boys how much she loved them and hated to leave them. A letter to Jane was next. The friendship she had found with her employer's sister was important to her.

When that difficult task had been completed,

Susannah rose to pace the room. The last letter was, of course, for Nicholas Danvers. She did not want to tell him goodbye. For the first time in her life, she had fallen in love. He was a good man, she told herself fiercely, who didn't deserve to be hurt, but today, because of her, he had almost lost his sons and his sister.

So she must say goodbye, without revealing her feelings, and yet tell him how much she appreciated his care, his warmth. New tears formed in her eyes as she remembered how frightened she'd been that first day in his library. Few men would have offered sanctuary to a young woman with a baby.

Not only had he done so, he had provided for her every need and made her and Cassandra feel a part of his family. Someday she would tell her daughter of the home they had left behind. And the man she loved so dearly.

She returned to the table and struggled with the words that would convey the proper feelings. A long time later she stood stiffly and folded each of the notes. As she did so, the door opened and Evie slipped into the room.

"Oh! I thought you be sleeping."

"No. I could not. Evie, could Cook send up a tray to my room just for this evening? I do not think I could compose myself to eat in front of the others."

"Why, o'course. Cook would bring it up herself if you asked. In the kitchen they'm be talking about how you saved Jem and Andy." Evie beamed at her mistress, as proud as if she herself were being praised.

"I—I did nothing. And Evie, could you ask Cook to send a large amount of food? I am extremely hun-

gry and—and I might want a snack later." Susannah
avoided the maid's eyes as she stumbled through her
request.

"Surely. Though I'm that surprised that you can
eat. Me, when I'm upset, I can't hardly keep my food
down."

"No, earlier I couldn't, either. Probably that is why
I am so hungry now."

With a click of her tongue Evie promised to bring
a tray at once and sped from the room. Susannah
stared at the closed door, wondering if she should
write a letter to Evie, also. But the maid could not
yet read very well, and she had asked Jane to tell
her goodbye for her. With a sigh she moved over
to the cabinet where she had hidden some of the
things she'd brought with her that first day. Silently
she examined the pistol hidden beneath a pile of
clothes.

It was one of her husband's dueling pistols. Fortunately, her aunt had had one of the stablehands
teach Susannah how to shoot when she was a young
girl. Aunt Molly had believed a woman should
know how to protect herself. Before Susannah left
her husband's estate, she'd taken one of his pistols for her protection. Now she needed it more
than ever.

Time seemed to be moving so slowly. She knew
she needed to rest because the trip she intended to
commence this evening would be long and exhaus-
ting, but she could not. Her mind constantly dwelled
on the horror of the afternoon.

She promised herself one last visit to the schoolroom to see her charges again. Perhaps now would
be the best time, and she could also collect

Cassandra from Colley. She wanted to keep her baby awake now so she would sleep later.

When she entered the schoolroom, Edward and Theodore rushed to meet her, their arms encircling her skirt. She returned their hugs and then sat down beside them.

"I wanted to tell you how proud I was of you both today. You did exactly as you were told. That was very important."

Theodore smiled at her, but Edward wore a frown on his face. "But we were supposed to protect you," he protested, "and you sent us away."

Susannah took his hand and said, "Yes, I did. I sent you with your aunt, who needed your protection more than I did."

"Oh." The little boy's face cleared as he thought over her words. "I wanted to help you."

"I know, darling, but following orders did help me. Are you both all right?"

"I'm fine," Theodore said. "We helped Colley with Cassie, too, and shared our special tea with her. Cook sent us gingerbread men!"

"Good. I'm going to collect Cassie now and go back downstairs, but I—I just want you both to know how much I love you." She gulped back the emotion rising in her. "Remember that I love you, no matter what happens."

They both hugged her neck and promised to remember, bewildered by her behavior. After she'd left, with Cassie, Edward explained to Theodore, "Adults act strange, sometimes, Teddy. But she'll be all right tomorrow."

She'd just reached her room with Cassandra in her arms when Evie arrived with a tray full of food.

Susannah settled Cassie in her cradle and sat down before the fire to eat.

"Cook wanted to send more when I ask for a big meal. She says you're a hero and should have whatever you want," Evie assured her, a broad smile on her face. "But I told her this would be enough."

Since the tray had ham, a roast chicken, various vegetables, cold quail, warm bread, and several desserts, Susannah agreed that it would be enough, even with the plans she had for it. "Thank you, Evie. Please tell Cook I appreciate her work."

She began eating while Evie did several chores in the room. After a few minutes, however, Susannah asked the maid to fetch her more bread from the kitchen. Evie looked up, surprised, to discover the bread plate empty.

"I can't resist Cook's fresh bread," Susannah said with a shrug. Evie hurried to do as she asked.

As soon as the door closed behind the maid, Susannah took a clean cloth and began to wrap whatever food she felt would be portable and remain fresh in it. She thought there might even be enough food to last her several days if she was careful, and she hoped to be almost to London by then.

Shoving the stuffed cloth under the bed, she straightened just as Evie reappeared. The maid started to put the bread on the tray and then stared in surprise. "My, you were really hungry," she said, turning to look at Susannah.

"Yes. And now I'm so stuffed, I think I'll go to bed early. After such a large meal, I'm sure I'll sleep late in the morning. If the squire does not mind, I think I'll not go to the schoolroom until tomorrow afternoon." The later they discovered her absence, the farther she would be away from the manor house.

"Shall I help you dress for bed?"

"No, thank you, Evie. I must tend to Cassie first. I'll manage on my own. Why don't you have an early night, also. You've certainly earned it."

After the maid expressed her gratitude and left the room, Susannah turned the lock and began her final preparations.

Peter and Nicholas scarcely conversed at all over dinner. Since the ladies remained in their bedchambers, the men were not forced to make conversation for its own sake. The events of the day had taken their toll on them as well as the ladies.

"Have you seen the boys?" Peter finally asked.

"Yes, I talked to them. They seem none the worse for the experience. Susannah had visited with them before me and reassured them."

"She certainly is good with them."

"Yes."

Moments passed as they ate their meal in silence. Finally Nicholas murmured, "I hope Susannah will tell us the truth tomorrow. She seems to be quite adept at keeping secrets."

"Perhaps if Jane and I are present, also—"

"You think she is less likely to lie to you than to me?" Nicholas asked, offended.

"No, Nick," Peter hastily assured him. "I only thought to put the odds in our favor. Three against one is better."

"Perhaps," Nicholas said with a shrug.

After their meal was ended, Nicholas suggested they adjourn to the library for their brandy. They were just getting comfortable when they heard a carriage in the drive followed by a loud knocking on the front door.

"Who would be arriving at this time of night?" Nicholas asked, but Peter had no answer. "Unless it is in response to the message I sent out to our neighbors." He hurriedly got to his feet.

Before he could reach the door, Pritchard opened it to admit a short, wiry man dressed in a black suit. "Sir," the butler said, "a Mr. Henry Amos to see you."

15

"Henry!" Peter cried out, rising to meet the man.

"My lord, I am glad to see you. Is Lady Craven here? Is she all right?"

The man earned Nicholas's approval at once since he exhibited a concern for Susannah's welfare. He answered the man's questions. "Yes, Lady Craven is here and is safe and sound. I am Nicholas Danvers."

"I am so relieved. When I received your letter, I decided the best thing was to hurry here to see her. Things have been in an uproar since I last saw her." He looked at the two men with anxious eyes.

"Be seated, Mr. Amos. I'll send for refreshments. In a few minutes I'll summon Lady Craven, also. But first there are some questions we would ask." He rang for Pritchard and ordered a tray before sitting down himself.

"Do you know why someone is trying to kill Lady Craven?" he asked as he rejoined the other two.

The man of business looked first at Lord Arbor, from whom he received an encouraging nod, and then Mr. Danvers. "Yes, sir, I believe I do." He coughed and then said, "I think I should tell you what I know from the beginning."

After receiving nods of agreement, he said, "You see, Lady Craven came to my office almost three months ago. She gave me a package to place in my safe, and she asked for a large sum of money. I thought it highly irregular, but, after all, it was her money." His brow furrowed again as he thought of such foolish behavior. "She told me she was going for a visit to her own estate. But then she said something peculiar, that I was not to advance any sum to her brother-in-law for any reason."

He paused and Nicholas and Peter leaned forward, as if urging him on. "Well, the present Lord Craven is not my favorite client, and I had no hesitation in promising her I would not do so. Then she left."

He coughed again and Nicholas wanted to grab him by his jacket and shake the information from him. However, Pritchard entered with a tray at that moment, and Nicholas had to be even more patient as the little man took a sip of tea.

"Just a few days later Lord Craven came to my office to inform me of the dowager Lady Craven's death." He took another sip of tea. "It was quite a shock, I can tell you. But I kept quiet, listening to his story. He concluded with the fact that he would be guardian to the child, so I should allow him an open budget to bring the estate up to date to provide a proper home for the child."

"He said he had the child?"

Mr. Amos looked at Nicholas in surprise. "Yes, of course. But then I asked him when Lady Craven had died, and the date he gave was a week before she came to see me. He said she'd been buried and all."

Nicholas remembered Susannah's cry in the stableyard about being responsible for another death. "Whose body was it?"

"I suspect her maid's. The woman has disappeared. When I informed Lord Craven that the dowager Lady Craven was still alive and had been seen by me and my entire staff after the date of burial, he became enraged. He so forgot himself as to demand where she might be found, thereby admitting he'd lied to me."

"So you think it is Lord Craven seeking her death? For the money he would control as guardian of the child?" Nicholas was anxious to get to the end of the story.

"Yes. Though I doubt the child would survive for long if he were the guardian."

Mr. Amos's simple statement sent a chill up Nicholas's back. No wonder Susannah was terrified. Her brother-in-law sounded a veritable monster. Nicholas sprang from his chair. "I will go ask Susannah to join us."

"But, Mr. Danvers—" Mr. Amos began, only to find himself talking to a closed door.

A darkly clad figure slipped from the basement door out into the darkness. Advancing toward the stables with great stealth, she paused several times to listen intently. Once, she patted her protruding front soothingly.

Finally reaching the stable doors, she lifted the latch carefully and swung open one door, halting with each squeak to see if she would be discovered. Several minutes later the figure reemerged leading the chestnut mare she always rode, the saddle in place. She led the horse to the mounting block and climbed up on it. But a small mew caused her to pause.

"Hush, Cassie," Susannah whispered, patting her swollen belly. Then she quickly checked the knot at her neck that formed the sling Cassie was snuggled into. The shawl was indeed a good idea. Cassie would be easy to carry and even easier to hide. After tying a bundle on the back of the saddle, Susannah then mounted and gathered the reins.

Sparing one moment to look wistfully at the home she and Cassie so loved, she then resolutely headed her mount down the drive, ignoring the tears streaming from her eyes. Perhaps it was those tears that kept her from noticing the dark form that stepped from behind the trees that lined the drive until he was in front of her, a shiny pistol gleaming in the moonlight.

Nicholas knew he should send for Susannah's maid to ask her to join them in the library, but he refused to do so. He ran up the stairs and knocked quietly on Susannah's bedchamber door. When there was no answer, he debated entering the room, but he feared such improper behavior would alarm his staff. He found a tweeny on her way upstairs and asked her to fetch Evie.

When Evie hurried up the back stairs, she found her master pacing the hallway. "Evie, your mistress appears to be sleeping. I cannot rouse her from knocking on the door. Go in and wake her."

"But, Master, she was very tired. Perhaps in the morning—"

"Evie, this cannot wait. It is about the shooting."
His stern tone convinced her as much as his words.

She slipped into the dark room and tiptoed to
the bed. "The master be at the door, wanting to talk
to you," she whispered. When there was no answer,
she reached out a hand to shake her shoulder. All
she touched was pillow. With a sinking feeling, she
felt around the bed, but there was no one there.
She ran to the door, crying, "Master, she be
gone!"

Nicholas pushed open the door, meeting Evie. He
quickly lit a candle from the mantel and carried it
to the bed. But as Evie had said, there was no one
there. Evie hurried to the cradle and found it empty, also.

As he swung around to leave, Nicholas noticed
several folded letters on the writing table. "When
did you last see her, Evie?"

"About an hour ago, Master. She said she was tired
and would go to bed as soon as the baby settled."
She bit back a sob. "Do you think someone has tak-
en her?"

"No, I think she decided to leave. Don't worry. I'll
bring her back," he assured her even as he rushed out
the door, the letters in his hand.

Afraid she already had a head start of an hour, he
ran down the stairs to the library. Swinging open the
door, he paused only long enough to say, "She's
gone. I'm going after her," before hurrying down
the backstairs.

After exchanging startled looks, the two men in
the library rushed out to follow him. All three
spilled out into the darkness and headed toward
the stables.

However, voices halted them.

"I thought ye might try to escape after t'day," a harsh voice said in the darkness.

"Please, don't harm us. I'll pay you whatever he offered and more."

Susannah's voice drew Nicholas like a magnet. Even though he was unarmed, he crept toward the dimly seen figure on horseback.

"I 'ave me honor, my lady. I gave me word."

"You consider it honorable to kill a woman and her child?"

Peter tapped Nicholas on the shoulder and pointed toward the trees on the other side of Susannah. He then slipped around Nicholas and crossed the drive.

"Ye'll not talk me out of it," the harsh voice continued, and he raised his arm.

"Wait!" Susannah cried.

"What for?" the scratchy voice asked. Even as he did so, fire spurted from Susannah's cloaked figure, and the boom of her pistol broke the silence, followed by a frightened shriek from Cassie.

"Susannah, wait!" Nicholas cried as he ran toward her. Peter came from behind the trees where he had tried to sneak past her attacker. Mr. Henry Amos followed closely behind Nicholas.

All three surrounded the mounted lady, taking her by surprise.

"Please, I must leave!" Susannah begged over Cassie's crying. "He will only send others. I won't endanger everyone. I can't!" Her plea did not win her release. Nicholas grabbed the reins of her horse.

"There is no need for you to run away. We'll find a way to help you," Nicholas assured her. He waved his stablehands, having come running at the sound of gunfire, toward the injured man on the ground.

"It's very simple," Mr. Amos said dryly. "I would've told you, Lady Craven, had you asked. I tried to tell Mr. Danvers, but he ran off to fetch you."

"Mr. Amos?" Susannah asked, peering into the darkness, wondering if she were dreaming.

"Yes, Lady Craven. Perhaps we could go back inside? It's very cold out here, and I've had a long trip."

His prosaic words relieved the tension. Several stablehands brought forward a lantern, and Nicholas instructed his minions to hold the attacker until the morrow. "Set up a guard. I want to see him first thing in the morning."

He reached up for the now whimpering Cassandra. "Hand down Cassie. Peter will take her."

Lord Arbor valiantly agreed to take the child, though he was inexperienced with babies. Having done so, he found she fit into his arms perfectly.

Nicholas then reached for Susannah, and she slid down into his arms. Though she was still confused by Mr. Amos's presence and his words, she did not object when Nicholas held her close. She had never felt more safe than when in his arms.

Mr. Amos coughed again. "Shall we go inside?"

Nicholas reluctantly released her, but he kept hold of her arm. He wasn't going to take a chance on her finding another way to slip from him.

When they entered the house, the servants were gathered at the door, having heard the shot, also. Nicholas took a moment to reassure them before the little party climbed the stairs. Evie, Lady Arbor, Theodore, and Edward were hovering on the stairs, trying to decide whether it was all right to come down.

"Susannah, you are safe!" Jane exclaimed and rushed down the few remaining steps to hug her friend. The boys followed in her footsteps. Evie, while delighted to see her mistress safe, immediately went to Lord Arbor's side to see about Cassandra.

"Everyone is safe," Nicholas said in exasperation. He did not want a crowd around. "Evie, take the baby back to her bed, please. Boys, back to—"

"But, Papa," Edward protested. "We want to know what happened. Why is Susannah dressed to go out when it is night? And with Cassie!"

With all the faces turned to plead with him, Nicholas threw up his hands. "Very well, everyone to the library. But once explanations are made, you are all to go to bed."

Even Evie slipped inside the room with the baby in her arms. She, too, wanted to know what had happened, and more important, what would happen on the morrow.

Mr. Amos's words only now seemed to penetrate Susannah's mind. "Mr. Amos, you said you could stop Gerald from—you have a solution?"

"Who is Gerald?" Jane asked.

Nicholas led Susannah to the sofa even as he answered. "Gerald is the present Lord Craven, Susannah's brother-in-law. It appears he was trying to kill Susannah to gain her inheritance."

Edward and Theodore broke from their places by the door to surround Susannah. Their father's stern look quieted their protests, but they clung to her for comfort.

"But if Susannah died, her estate would go to Cassandra," Jane protested before her eyes widened. "You mean he would even kill a baby?"

"Darling, I think Susannah is anxious to hear what Mr. Amos has to say. Perhaps we'll ask questions later." Peter received a grateful look from Nicholas.

Susannah turned to her man of business. "Mr. Amos?"

"My dear Lady Craven, if you had only consulted me, I could have told you the solution to your difficulties. All that was required was a will leaving your estate to someone other than your brother-in-law in the event of yours and Cassandra's deaths."

Stunned by the simplicity of his answer, Susannah simply stared at him. Nicholas asked, "That would have stopped his attempts to murder her?"

"Why not? He would not benefit from her death in such an event. Why risk being charged with murder for nothing?"

The man's words made sense to everyone.

"But he will be charged with murder now," Nicholas added firmly. "I am the local magistrate, and I will question our prisoner in the morning. Will you be able to take his statement to the proper authorities in London?"

"Of course." He looked at his client. "Tomorrow, you may give me your orders for your new will, and your difficulties will be over."

"Thank you, Mr. Amos." A sudden thought occurred to Susannah. "But why are you here?"

"Mr. Danvers wrote to me. As soon as I learned your whereabouts, I hurried to see you. Lord Craven had already tried to convince me you were dead."

Everyone simply stared at him. He stood. "Mr. Danvers, would it be possible for me to retire now? I've been traveling night and day to arrive as soon as possible, and I find myself exhausted."

"Of course." Nicholas summoned Pritchard.

After the man of business had left the library, Nicholas murmured, "A most unflappable gentleman."

"How did you know—" Susannah began.

"It is a long story. It is late. Why don't you also retire. Now that your problem is solved, there is no rush."

"But Susannah isn't going away, is she?" Edward cried, having followed the events enough to fear such an occurrence.

That was a question to which Nicholas didn't want to hear an answer. At least not yet. But everyone else in the room was looking at Susannah.

"I—I don't know. I don't want to go, Edward, but your father—"

"Papa!" both boys protested.

"Nick, surely you would not—" Jane began.

"Master, couldn't she stay?" Evie cried.

"*I* have not asked her to leave!" Nicholas roared. "But she is an heiress and not in need of a position."

"You mean because she has money she cannot live with us?" Edward asked.

Theodore pressed more closely against Susannah. "Can't you give it away?" he pleaded, his eyes, so like his father's, full of tears.

She wrapped her arms around him and looked up at Nicholas, unable to answer.

He stared down at her before abruptly turning away. "Do not be ridiculous, Teddy," he said harshly.

Jane moved to the sofa to sit beside Susannah and take Teddy's hand again. "Darling, Susannah cannot simply live here with you unless she has a position, which she doesn't need, or—" She paused to look first at Susannah and then her brother, her eyes dancing with mischief. "Or unless she married your father and became your mother." Amid the boys' enthusiastic acceptance of such an event, Jane threw her brother a challenging look, and he glared at her in return.

Susannah gasped and ducked her head after one quick look at Nicholas's anger. Pandemonium reigned for several minutes as both children pleaded with their father for him to follow their aunt's suggestion.

"Enough!" Nicholas roared. Absolute silence followed his shout. "Lady Craven must decide her future. She has wealth and position. She does not need to live far away from London and society."

Susannah drew a deep breath. She had fought for her safety, hers and Cassandra's. She could do no less for her happiness. "I don't want to live in London."

Nicholas looked at her, a light in his eyes that she could not interpret. "You don't?"

"No, I want to live here." She watched him closely, afraid she would see the anger he had already shown.

"But then you'd have to marry Papa," Edward reminded her.

"I know." Her blue eyes were full of the love she felt for Nicholas Danvers. She only hoped he wanted that love.

He stared at her, drinking in her beauty, before he whispered, "Susannah!" Swiftly he sank to one knee in front of her. "Susannah, you are sure? I cannot live in London. I don't even care to visit it often."

"She said she doesn't want to live there, Papa," Theodore assured him. "Didn't you hear?"

Ignoring his son, he reached out a hand to cup her soft cheek. "And I hate secrecy and lies," he whispered. "I would demand your honesty."

Susannah covered his hand with hers. "I only have one secret left, Nicholas." He waited silently, his brown eyes never leaving her blue ones. "I am full of love, for you and your children, but it has been hidden in my heart for a long time. I love you, Nicholas." He closed his eyes, and Susannah held her breath, afraid he did not love her in return. She didn't have long to wait, however. With a jubilant shout, he stood and scooped her up into his arms, his lips covering hers.

The family shouted their excitement, which drew Pritchard to the library door. "Sir? Is there aught amiss?" he asked as he opened the door. The sight of his master kissing Mrs. Brown reduced him to silence.

"Mr. Pritchard! The master is going to marry Mrs. Brown!" Evie told him eagerly.

"She's going to be our mother!" Edward added.

"I think it might be wise if we all left them alone," Peter said, pulling his wife up from the sofa. "Boys, back to bed. Evie, care for Cassie, and Pritchard, do not disturb them, please. Tomorrow, we will all celebrate together."

Within minutes the library was silent. Nicholas finally lifted his head and whispered, "We are alone."

"Yes," Susannah agreed, a delightful smile covering her face. "Oh, Nicholas, I cannot believe we are safe and you love me."

"I think I have loved you since you first stepped foot into this room, you with your baby hidden in your basket."

"But you kept trying to send me away!" she protested.

"No, I did not. But I feared you would not want to stay. You are so beautiful that I could not believe—"

She placed her fingers over his lips. "You must believe, dear heart. You have taken away my secrets and given me love in return. I cannot imagine a more happy trade."

"Nor can I, my love, nor can I."

And he proved it with his kiss.